PRAISE FOR *ART OF CAMOUFLAGE*

"From military training and the camouflage that protects, to the masks we wear to conceal flaws even to ourselves, Sara Power comes out swinging with a gripping debut with characters caught between ache and outrage. A wildly imaginative and welcome new voice."

SHELAGH ROGERS founding host and co-creator of The Next Chapter, CBC Radio

"In *Art of Camouflage*, Sara Power courageously depicts military life, yet there isn't a single battlefield in these pages. Instead, Power invites us into the overlooked lives of military wives, discombobulated recruits, and children growing up on bases, for whom every home is temporary and every friendship destined to be severed. Fiercely intelligent, funny and tender, *Art of Camouflage* is a remarkable debut."

CAROLINE ADDERSON author of *A Russian Sister* and *Ellen in Pieces*

"In this exhilarating debut, Sara Power uses her considerable gifts to illuminate lives touched by the military. Touching, funny, and often absurd, each of these short stories contains a whole world."

ALIX OHLIN author of *We Want What We Want* and *Dual Citizens*

"Sara Power's *Art of Camouflage* is full of complex characters who make costly miscalculations, and wear masks that reveal more than they hide. They endure and know when to quit; they're vulnerable and tremble with rage; peacekeepers walking the tightrope of misogyny. Power's prose is lightning quick, making the dark that follows illumination even darker. Shot through with brilliant images and an elegant fluidity, these stories are striking, subtle, and ultimately spectacular."

LISA MOORE author of *This Is How We Lo*

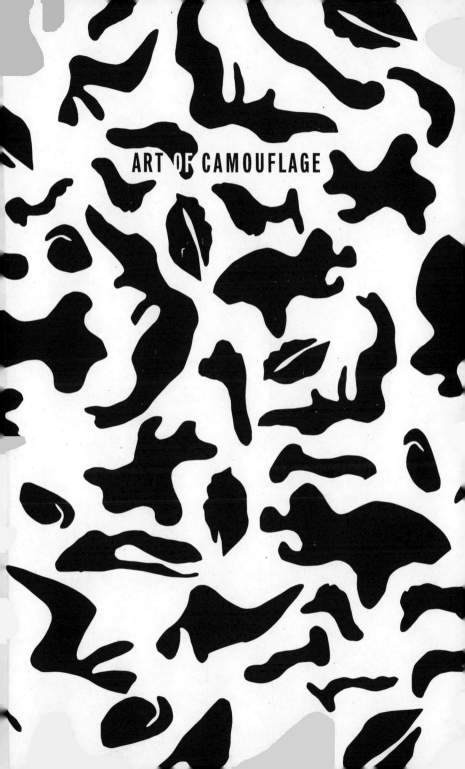

ART OF CAMOUFLAGE

ART OF CAMOUFLAGE

STORIES

SARA POWER

Freehand Books gratefully acknowledges the financial support for its publishing program provided by the Canada Council for the Arts and the Alberta Media Fund, and by the Government of Canada through the Canada Book Fund.

This book is available in print and Global Certified Accessible™ EPUB formats.

Freehand Books is located in Moh'kinsstis, Calgary, Alberta, within Treaty 7 territory and Métis Nation of Alberta Region 3, and on the traditional territories of the Siksika, the Kainai, and the Piikani, as well as the Iyarhe Nakoda and Tsuut'ina nations.

FREEHAND BOOKS
freehand-books.com

Library and Archives Canada Cataloguing in Publication
Title: Art of camouflage : stories / Sara Power.
Names: Power, Sara, author.
Identifiers:
  Canadiana (print) 20240286839
  Canadiana (ebook) 20240286847
  ISBN 9781990601675 (softcover)
  ISBN 9781990601682 (EPUB)
  ISBN 9781990601699 (PDF)
Subjects: LCGFT: Short stories.
Classification: LCC PS8631.O85 A78 2024 | DDC C813/.6 — dc23

Edited by Naomi K. Lewis
Design by Natalie Olsen
Author photo by Curtis Perry
Printed and bound in Canada

Earlier versions of the stories in this collection were originally published in the following: *The Bath Short Story Award Anthology:* "About Face." *The Malahat Review:* "The Circular Motion of a Professional Spit-Shiner" and "Pangaea Fragmented." *Riddle Fence:* "Kijiji BFF." *The New Quarterly:* "Art of Camouflage." *Prairie Fire Magazine:* "G-LOC." *Canthius:* "Roe v. Caviar." *Room Magazine:* "Lifted." *The Toronto Star:* "Half-life." *Minola Review:* "Christmas Card for the Win." *Carve Magazine:* "Portrait of a Mother." *Hunger Mountain Review — Vermont College of Fine Arts Journal of the Arts:* "A Pessoa Guide to a Birthday." Quotations in "A Pessoa Guide to a Birthday" are from *The Book of Disquiet* by Fernando Pessoa, translated by Margaret Jull Costa (Serpent's Tail, 1991).

SECOND PRINTING

Canada   Canada Council for the Arts   Conseil des Arts du Canada   Albertan Government

FOR MY MOTHER,
AND HER MOTHER,
AND THEIR MULTITUDES.

CONTENTS

ART
OF
CAMOUFLAGE

ABOUT FACE

Nine months ago, in early December of last year, my best friend and Johnson's Insurance cubicle neighbour, Lexi, had a sleepover. Just the girls, she said. Wear pjs. No bras. We'll drink rosé, soak nude in the hot tub, research vaginal beads, buff our heels, and so on. Me, you, Mags, and Rita.

My husband had just left for a year-long deployment to Bahrain. My son was sleeping at his friend's house. I was game.

We applied purifying face masks.

Mags's face mask was an elf with red circles for cheekbones and right-angled eyebrows that gave her a fixed expression of shock. Rita's mask was a melancholy snowman, white-faced with black rings around the eyes that made her look like a geisha. Lexi was Santa with a white textured beard and moustache, and I had a shiny red nose with pointy antlers flaring from my forehead. When it was time to remove the masks, we peeled the slimy film, massaged the goop to exfoliate impurities, and rinsed. Everyone was shiny and clean except for me. The red nose and antlers remained as if carbon copied onto my skin.

"Use this almond oil," Lexi said, laughing. "Looks like Rudolph has more colour saturation."

We all laughed, but the more I tried to remove the mask from my face, the more the reindeer features developed. The white antlers on my forehead deepened into a rich beige, and a triangle of brown appeared between my eyebrows, extending down the bridge of my nose to the ruby red circle at its tip. By midnight, after verifying expiration dates and soaking and oiling and exfoliating my face, a fully articulated Rudolph appeared to have been baked onto my skin. It was as though the mask had cured.

The following morning in my apartment, my efforts to conceal my face with makeup were unsuccessful. I blotted and dabbed layers upon layers of cover-up until the texture of my skin resembled that of crushed velvet. The red nose would not be concealed. The antlers had formed crevices that looked like welts or burn scars when caked with makeup. My eyes were bloodshot and sunken. Staring out from beneath the glare of fluorescent light was a miserable distortion of my face; I hardly recognized myself.

"Whoa, Mom, your face!" Mick stood behind me in the bathroom mirror. "You're so puffy," he said. "Are you like, sick or something?" He shifted his headphones from his ears to his neck. "You should lie down, Mom, or take a bath. Your face is messed up."

"It's just this mask thing gone wrong," I said, concealing my distress with earnest aplomb. "I'm good, sweetie. Yes, bath, good, good. How was Min-jae's?"

"Awesome. Stayed up till two in the morning playing Minecraft. You have to see the house I built."

After a long ineffective bath, I spent the better part of the afternoon as a guest in Mick's virtual world in which he'd built a sprawling four-story, glass-ceilinged house. With a plethora of spheres, wedges, cylinders, and prisms, he built custom fixtures. He guided me through a system of steps he had devised to make an air-hockey table — shrinking wedges into goal posts, positioning cylinders for table legs, altering colour filters to emit neon lights, affixing pressure plates to produce the buzzing sound of victory. He showed me how to build a dumpster, zeroing the transparency of an interior block to achieve a hollowed-out appearance. Secret tunnels and passageways connected his house to those of his friends. There were sinkholes hidden behind mock fireplaces, secret doors in bookshelves and closets, a hidden ladder descending from a water fountain. He aligned blocks that produced electrical currents capable of opening doors, moving pistons, activating dispensers, rotating gears. His sense of industry and inventiveness was astounding. He could generate infinite sources of power.

"People who troll other people in Minecraft are called *griefers*," he explained. "They can fill your house with TNT or lava then Poof! Gone. In like, three seconds — *gone!* Total devastation. I hate griefers," he said. "I set traps for them."

. . . .

Over the holidays, people applauded what they thought was vigorous holiday spirit. "B, your mask is method," said Norm at the office party. "Just last month, I took Careen to the Winnipeg Ballet, where all the dancers wore masks. Woodland creatures, you know? Except for Evelyn Hart, she was the only ballerina without a mask. They choreographed a role just for her. She is sixty-two but still a total rockstar; I mean limber as fuck. Her body is like sinew, you know. She kept running back and forth on this table and they were constantly lifting her." Norm raised his hands, imaginary lifting. "Honestly, if they dropped her, she would have like, crumbled, like, she would have broken a hip for sure." He sipped his rum and Coke. "Of course, Careen loved it. Said the entire ballet was like being in a place where you might fall off a precipice or something. Careen loves weird shit."

Instead of fading, the mask got darker and more pronounced. Thick brown facial hair sprouted around my eyes, reducing my peripheral vision to zero. In cold wind, the red nose glowed like a beacon. I could have guided ships to harbour. Obviously, I was deeply perplexed by these dramatic changes to my face. I didn't tell my husband. What could he do from Bahrain? Not to mention, I preferred to keep things quiet on the home front. I called the cosmetic company, Zen Effect Health and Beauty, and they said I may have an allergy to the coalescing agents used in the mask. The results of the mask vary from person to person and according to age and skin type, they advised. They gifted me two complimentary pairs of exfoliating gloves.

At first, I admit, I felt more seen than ever, the double takes, the lingering stares, but gradually, the stares turned into mutual feelings of discomfort and shame. Anxious glances flashed and averted. Parents on the subway whispered to their children that it was rude to point. Sustained eye contact became something of my past. Even Lexi and the girls were aloof. Lexi felt responsible and guilty, even though I believed her when she said she had never intended to do this to me. The people closest to you can inflict the most permanent damage. Preach, sister!

I don't go out with them anymore. I have binge-watched *Succession* and *Killing Eve* and *Fleabag*, and have made a substantial dent in *The Witcher*. I'm trying to embrace my new reality.

"Mom, I'd prefer if you didn't go to parent/teacher night with your Rudolph face. Can you say you can't make it?"

"Oh! Yeah, sure, sweetie. I'll send an email."

I was the epitome of cool and collected.

I threw myself into my work, which thankfully involves phone conversations such as, *We would like to remove our daughter from our policy. She's off to California for college, so proud. Do you have kids?* Or *We downsized to a condo. Purged aggressively, donated our baby grand to Linehan's Assisted Living,* or *Can I please remove sewer back-up protection from our plan because, well, my husband has been diagnosed with lupus and can't work, and doesn't have workers' comp. Times are tough.* I started to eat lunch at my desk. I skipped Friday socials. I had groceries delivered.

"It's not like you have an actual disability, though," Lexi offered from her cubicle, "and you still have your job, your benefits. You have your pension. You have a great figure, B. Look at your teeth, for God's sake, they are so straight, and Mick. Mick is the best kid ever," she said.

"Right? I mean, it's pathetic that I even complain about my face."

. . . .

At the end of July, Mick and I packed up and road-tripped east for my cousin's wedding. We made a playlist and called it *Summer Habitz.*

"So, are you ever going to do anything about your face, Mom?" Mick asked while playing Bastion on his tablet in the passenger seat.

"There's nothing I can do, Mick," I said. "My face is my face."

"Isn't there a product or something?"

"A magical product?" Heavy sigh. "No, Mick, there is no magical product."

"Don't you hate the stares?"

"I mean, I don't love it, obviously," I said. "I'm getting used to it, I guess. It could be worse, you know."

"It could not be worse, Mom."

"Actually, it could be worse, Mick."

"Whatever."

At my cousin's wedding, people pretended not to notice my new face. Like Uncle Donald when he asked, "So, B, what's new with you?"

"Well, not much, Uncle Donald. I have a Rudolph face. Check out my shiny red nose." I didn't say this. I said, Yes, he's doing well in school. Yes, he still loves BMX. No, no serious girlfriend yet. Downhill losing battle with devices. Jake will be home from Bahrain in a few months. Crazy how time flies.

Not one person asked about my face, even when the nose glowed like a neon sign that blinks, *Come in, we're open.*

. . . .

I thought a movie night might provide an opportunity for Mick and me to bond. "I'll make pizza?"

"Not tonight, Mom. I'm gonna chill at Min-jae's."

"Hey Mick, wanna walk with me to the mailbox?"

"Not now, Mom. I'm playing on Roblox with Min-jae and Logan."

"Mick? A&W?"

"Actually, Mom. I'm meeting Min-jae at The Yard. Drive me?"

"Mick? You there? Mick?"

Nope.

....

Mick asked me why I have to be such a weirdo. Why would I put something like that on my face in the first place? Am I trying to be modern? And why do I listen to Chance the Rapper? Am I trying to humiliate him?

"You know what," I opined while mincing ginger, "when you compartmentalize the sexism, his music is quite expansive."

"Really, Mom? Wow! I just can't. You're killing me, Mom. I will seriously die. I can't even handle you right now."

This morning, while we ate breakfast together, Mick gave me a lesson on parenting etiquette. He said he hated the way I adopted an ultra-casual attitude when his friends are around. "For example," he said, "please stop using the word 'sick.' Like when sick means cool. Please stop using sick in that context. It's embarrassing."

"Don't be embarrassed, Mick. You can't help that your momma is *sick*."

Mick pushed his chair back and stood up, knocking the table, sloshing milk from his bowl of cereal. "*See?*" he said, towering over me. "You are ridiculous. And with your face like that? I am not joking, Mom, you are wrecking my life. I am not joking."

"You know what? I don't have to take you to the skatepark."

"Fine. Don't."

"Fine."

So here I am on my couch on a gorgeous Saturday afternoon, day-drinking by myself. Around this time last year, or maybe it was later in September, pre-Rudolph face anyway, I was sitting on a bench at the skatepark playing Alto's Odyssey on my phone while Mick zipped around. Jake was in Trenton completing work-up training for his deployment. I'd made egg sandwiches and put ice cubes in our water bottles. Mick and I sat on the bench together and ate our lunch.

"Mom," he said. "Addy makes videos of these squishy toys that she finds all beaten up at Value Village. She sands them down and patches them up and repaints them like new, and she has over three thousand subscribers."

"Squishies?" I asked.

"Yeah, like these little squish toys."

"Is she your girlfriend?"

"I like her."

"Do you see her outside of school?"

"She BMXs. She's like, sick. Really well known at the track."

When he finished his sandwich, Mick stood next to me for a few moments watching the other kids on the skatepark.

He clasped his hands behind his back, and I remember thinking he looked like a little old man, quiet and contemplative. It was sweet, and it gave me a dreamy feeling. Then he scratched his forearm, leaving white flaky tracks on his skin.

....

At my work, all calls are monitored in order to optimally manage the customer/agent relationship. Voice-analysis algorithms detect heightened emotional states, sentiment, and mood. Key words coupled with tonal range indicate distress, or anger, or customer dissatisfaction. Patterns of non-fluid speech, one-sided conversations, and silence can indicate the probability of customer abandonment. I think about the algorithms that might be assigned to the conversations I have with my son; I think about abandonment.

I think about pressure points and sinkholes and lava.

At my work, agents receive feedback on conversations in real time. A small coffee icon pops up when a break is due within the upcoming call cycle. A tiny blinking yield sign indicates a proclivity for run-on sentences. The appearance of an oak tree denotes the presence of frustration and prompts an agent to revisit learned strategies of mindfulness in order to achieve a more desirable empathy factor. As I sit here on a Saturday afternoon, day-drinking by myself, I imagine pop-up icons that might respond to my current experience of a hollow tree. A flood of thermometers rolls before my eyes. A chick in an egg, an eight ball, joysticks and hole-in-one flags, a carrot stick, a cactus, a tiny tornado spewing dust. Roller coaster, barber pole, taxicab, satellite, a conveyor belt of identical cubes of TNT.

Poof!

....

My eyebrows are now almost two-and-a-half inches thick. I know this because I measured them. I know that I am losing my son; he drifts further from me every day. Although it aggravated my sense of abandonment, I bought him a public transit pass so that he can take the bus to the skatepark. I have accepted that there is nothing I can do to stop his drift. I have decided that trying to prevent it would be like trying to stop the leaves from turning red and orange and lime green.

There is cheerful news, however. In yoga class last night, from the depths of my pigeon pose, which has improved dramatically in the past nine months, I noticed another woman, also deep in pigeon. I was drawn to her throughout the entire class, the way she moved between postures. Her strength and flexibility were something to behold. Her openness. So enthralled was I with her limber transitions, I decided to approach her after class to tell her how much I admired her practice, her grace. At first, I thought it was the dim light, a shadow, or sweat perhaps, but no, it was a patch of black hair on her chin. Vertical stripes of black and white hair covered her cheeks, then parted to form a diamond of black and white

13

at her forehead. The woman had the strikingly beautiful face of a zebra. We stared at each other, and then, without a word, we hugged. We hugged like it was a shipwreck. We held each other for a long time, and I could feel her pulse, or maybe it was my pulse. I have no idea.

THE CIRCULAR MOTION OF A
PROFESSIONAL SPIT-SHINER

Joyce is practicing her tightrope mime routine. Suppresses her bounce with a tilt of her pelvis as she lifts her right foot to advance on the tightrope. There is no rope, of course. The sound of a bagpipe practice chanter seeps through the dormitory walls. Roy is practising his scales.

A care package from her dad arrived last week. *Love Dad,* the card says. *Congrats! You made it through first year, xoxo.* Oreos, Oh Henry! Bars, Skittles. His scratchy handwriting makes Joyce pang for home, and she opens a package of Oreos. Sitting at her desk, she flips through her college handbook, pausing on a vintage photograph of The Old 18 — the first eighteen gentlemen cadets to enter the Royal Military College in 1876. In the photograph, the gentlemen cadets wear pillbox hats with black chin straps indenting their cheeks, scarlet doeskin tunics embroidered in gold, brass buttons descending their fronts. Like wind instruments, she thinks, as she eats another cookie whole. The gentlemen cadets' uniforms are identical to the one she'll wear on graduation parade in two weeks. It still doesn't feel real to her.

There's another bagpiper now. Outside in the distance, the piercing hum floods over the college grounds. Almost every evening, Fourth-Year Gibbs plays his bagpipes on the pier, droning ancient, far-off melodies over the man-made Navy Bay, across the parade square, past the clock tower of Currie Hall and Fort Frederick and the inner field. It penetrates Lasalle dormitory and Joyce's room, creating a triangulation of her position and Roy next door, and Gibbs on the pier, with his raucous lamentation.

Last September, when she first entered her quarters in the Lasalle building, it struck her how plain the interior was compared to the Tudor entranceway and the parapeted side gables and buttresses of the exterior. She had imagined ornate ceilings and stairwells, but the interior was more echo chamber than gothic collegiate. Acoustics absorbed into quadrangles of carpeted hallways and squat rooms. Austere, grey, uniform spaces. The place still feels austere and grey to her, except for Roy. Roy is an infinite source of generosity, she thinks, as he bleats through the opening bars of "Scotland the Brave."

Joyce stands and braces her body to walk across the tight-rope. It's not that she has to make herself believe she is on a tightrope; she has to make herself forget the tightrope isn't there. Leaning over her sink, she forces her fingers down her throat, bringing up clods of Oreo, sweet and bitter. She rinses her mouth and washes her hand.

....

The first six weeks at RMC are known as recruit term, a gruelling period of initiation when recruits are under the constant supervision of select third-year officer cadets. Joyce and Roy stood side by side during daily inspection and she recognized something particular about his scent — something dank and familiar, like the morning scent of a sibling. He had shadowy temples and a concave chest, was incapable of remembering drill commands or historical dates, could barely manage ten push-ups, and limped behind on morning runs. In the evenings, recruits were penalized with *circles* for failing to meet designated standards. Recruit flights formed up on the side of the parade square to watch the under-performers sprint the perimeter. Roy ran circles almost every evening, his skinny legs gangly and puppet-like, his eyes fixed on the ground.

Recruit room layout included hospital-cornered beds, socks rolled into ovals, shirts folded ten inches by ten inches. On the shelf above the sink, a bar of soap, a razor, deodorant, toothpaste, and a toothbrush were aligned and spaced according to the manual. The sink had to be dry; the trash can, empty. Recruit staff arrived at zero-five-hundred-hours to storm the quarters with white gloves and rulers. When Third-Year Nadeau found a red pubic hair on Roy's bar of soap, she held it in front of his face. "Disgusting," she had barked. Part of the inspection layout was a framed photo of a loved one, and Roy displayed his sister, who was an Olympic rower. His nickname became the Olympian.

Third-Year Nadeau was one of three female recruit staff in the entire college of almost twelve hundred officer cadets. She had been a competitive gymnast in high school and could do endless chin-ups. She was short and slim and wore her hair in a tightly weaved French braid that drew her face taut. During one morning inspection, Third-Year Nadeau found a dead fly on Joyce's windowsill. "You will carry this fly in your left hand for the day, Recruit Dunning," she announced. "You will explain to anyone who asks that your attention to detail is poor, and that you are incapable of serving your country, or this fly." At the dining hall that evening, the fly had morphed into a slick bean in Joyce's hand, its wings and legs rubbed away.

....

BY THE RIGHT ___ QUICK ___ MARCH. It's graduation parade practice and the Cadet Wing Training Officer yells drill commands over the bagpipes. As Joyce marches in file, she feels a fleeting connection to something giant and historic.

The precision, the synchronization, the percussive sound of boots on pavement like a collective pulse. First-Year Pellerin is in front of her in file, and she notices his neck, can see the razor burn there. During recruit term, Pellerin joked about how small Third-Year Nadeau's tits were. *She loves cock,* he had whispered to the others. BY THE LEFT___ RIGHT___ TURN. Pellerin's drill is flawless, and in her peripheral vision, Joyce watches his gait and extends her step to match. She imagines a board connecting the base of her skull to her tailbone, a technique she acquired in mime that works in situations which demand both rigidity and flexion.

It was Roy who introduced Joyce to mime. Back in October, during their first free weekend after recruit term, dressed in their navy blue, number-four uniforms, they marched off the college grounds, saluting the Memorial Arch as they passed.

TRUTH DUTY VALOUR
Blow out your bugles over the rich dead
There's none of these so lonely and poor of old
But dying has made us rarer gifts than gold.

Princess Street shops were bustling, and Joyce had a keen sense of her surroundings. It was her first time being in uniform in public, and it might have been another dimension. Never in her life had she felt so seen; she paid close attention to her posture.

They entered a cafe on Brock Street called The Moth and found themselves in the middle of a mime open mic. When seated, they ordered two towering pieces of raspberry cheesecake.

"There are two fourth-year cadets I mix up every time," Roy said. "Johnston from Six Squadron and Lee from Two."

"They're not alike at all," Joyce said.

"They remind me of huskies. Husky dogs."

"I see it," Joyce said, savouring a mouthful of cheesecake.

"Truth, Duty, Valour!" Roy raises his glass, mocking. "Some fourth-years shit in the leopard-crawl obstacle, you know," he said with his mouth full. "After a night at AJs, loaded, they shit in the mud that we had to crawl through."

It was that sort of baseness, something feral and bleak, that had started to engulf Joyce. She felt like the other cadets had a preternatural knowledge of military life and their course within it, while Joyce felt like she was floating and aimless. The hierarchies were oppressive to her, and the RMC brand of ambition lacked the dexterity she craved. She had no bearings. A chasm existed between her original notions of RMC and the reality of her experience. With each passing week, she imagined something inside of her smudging away.

On that first night at The Moth, Roy walked to the stage and performed a short skit, miming a waiter in a diner, getting hoots of laughter when he whipped imaginary customers with an imaginary dishcloth. Joyce's fascination with mime was born. Something clicked into place for her. She liked the silent mode of suggestion offered in mime. Instead of commands and orders and the forcing of will, mime asked for understanding in a playful, malleable way.

It was the first time she threw up her food, that night at The Moth, and the emptying left her with a sense of satisfaction. A sense of an altered self—not a self that might fit into this military life she had chosen, but one that could release her from time to time—a self she could control in this elemental way.

....

On the parade square, they march past the dais. TO THE RIGHT ___ SALUTE. As she turns her head and snaps her hand to her temple, it comes to her. The song rushes into her with all its airy notes, its lust and lucidity. It was Seal. It was Seal's "Kiss from a Rose," and his hands firm and hot on her waist. Fourth-Year Gibbs had stared at her with such intensity she might have mistaken it for devotion. "What the fuck is someone like you doing in a place like this?" he had said. EYES ___ FRONT.

....

Later that evening, Joyce and Roy are polishing their parade boots together in the cadet common room with her dad's care package between them on the floor.

"Take one," she says, throwing an Oh Henry! Bar at him. "Take them all, please."

"Merci beaucoup, mon amie," Roy says as the bar bounces off his knee. "My parents and sister arrive tomorrow."

"The Olympian!"

"Sherri doesn't compete anymore," Roy says. "She retired after Atlanta. Her body couldn't take it." His mouth yawns open as he breathes on the toe of his boot, readjusting the yellow Kiwi cloth around his pointer and middle fingers, polishing in small circles the way Joyce had shown him. "So, did you hear about Fourth-Year Gibbs?"

Joyce shakes her head, eating Skittles one by one.

"He fell!" Roy says with a grin. "He fell on parade today. Hungover. Broke his wrist. He's off grad parade, and Fourth-Year Newman is lead piper now."

Joyce squirrels her own hand inside her boot and holds it up, the glassy shine like the black of a lake. Her face stares back, disproportioned and creaturely.

"Karma," Roy says.

"Roy," Joyce says abruptly. "What's that on my pillow?" Roy had placed her pillow behind his back, and she can see a smear of orange across it.

"Man," he groans. "Fake tanner — sorry."

"Fake tanner? Are you serious?"

"It enhances muscle tone."

"Wow," Joyce says, packing up her stuff. "K, I'm done, Fabio.

Feel free to stay here until you're finished. I'm going for a run."

"You're insane."

"You're orange, Roy. Orange," she says, laughing. "Just grab me a new pillowcase, please and thank you."

Outside, Joyce takes off at a clip past the adjacent dormitories of Lasalle and Haldimand. There's a hint of fresh paint from the bleachers on the inner field, and she runs past the stone wall of Fort Frederick and cuts across the grass to the St. Lawrence River. Lights of Kingston reflect on the water and the Wolfe Island Ferry is docking. She can hear the drone of a vehicle as it crosses the Kingston bridge. Gibbs, she thinks, imagining his fall on the parade square, his bagpipes deflating and droning beneath his crumpled body.

....

Every year in October, the end of recruit term is celebrated with a college-wide party where beer is sold by the pitcher. Within the first hour, most cadets have removed their beer-soaked shirts. After six weeks of no eye contact with anyone outside her recruit flight, Joyce was met with an entirely new set of faces. There were only a handful of first-year girls, and everyone knew who she was. She felt the eyes on her. It was exhilarating.

On the dance floor, a tall, lean, shirtless guy grabbed her wrist, smiling. Another cadet with his shirt wrapped around his head grabbed her other wrist. They pressed in close, and she danced between them. The first guy looked down at Joyce's body attentively, examining her. He linked his hands around her lower back and moved loosely with the music, closing his eyes, as if entering a fantasy that had nothing to do with her. She liked it. She liked his vacuous state, his bitter, musky scent. The second guy was behind her, in sync, the three of them folding into one another, reciprocating.

It was when they were joined by Fourth-Year Gibbs that the harmony was disrupted. A crude number nine painted on his chest, Gibbs wedged himself between them. The first guy stiffened, but continued to dance as Gibbs wrapped his shirt around Joyce's neck. He was playful, shimmying into her as he manoeuvred the shirt down her back. Placing his hands firmly on her waist, he yelled down at her, "What the fuck is someone like you doing in a place like this?" He tied the damp shirt around her head so tightly, her earrings cut into her neck. She was blindfolded. She tried to wrestle the shirt from her face, but it wouldn't come off. Bodies closed in around her. Hands mauled her stomach, her armpits. Fingers pressed and prodded between her legs. She pulled and pawed at the blindfold as hands grabbed her breasts and a hard cock pressed into her back. Lashing out, she flailed, smacking at the bodies that surrounded her as a pitcher of cold beer was dumped over her head.

Joyce bit down hard on her tongue and lost her balance, falling into a greasy, slick chest, then to the floor. On the floor, she tugged at the blindfold until it released. Her head was spinning, the skin on her face was raw, and around her, a small circle of shirtless guys was uncurious as they backed away. She walked off the dance floor and the circle that had formed closed in and disappeared.

. . . .

Joyce picks up her pace as she sprints around Point Frederick Drive, the taste of Skittles on the roof of her mouth. The Wolfe Island ferry is making its way to the island now. Back at Fort Frederick, she opens the large wooden door and enters, where the giant belly of a Martello tower looms over grassy banks that form an arrowhead. Barrels of gunpowder were once stored within these earthworks, and after the recruit obstacle course, she and the other members of her flight had stood in single file inside the dark, musty tunnels, taking turns drinking some unknown sludge, reciting one by one, a quote from the college's first Commandant:

> *Valour, gentlemen as the heritage of the grand old*
> *stock from which we are all sprung. If you are true,*
> *if duty is your star, you are sure to be brave.*
> *Truth Duty Valour*

Her face is sweating. With one hand on her knee, she roots her fingers down her throat, emptying herself of Skittles.

. . . .

The following day, first-, second-, and third-year cadets are given the afternoon off while the graduating class rehearses the presentation of commissioning scrolls.

"Wanna book kayaks on Navy Bay?" Roy suggests.

"Not really," Joyce says.

"Let's take the ferry to Wolfe Island then," he says. "C'mon, we've been talking about doing it all year."

Joyce agrees, and they walk into Kingston, sharing whiskey from Roy's flask.

"I can't stop thinking about Gibbs," he says. "Missing his own grad parade." He takes a drink. "You know, I heard some of the other pipers talk about how fucked up he is. He has issues, I think. Like he's not right in the head."

As the ferry passes the peninsula and RMC campus, Joyce stares at the tidy quadrangles of limestone buildings. The patina of copper rooftops is a serene shade of green. Curry Hall, its stained-glass windows and clock tower. Archaic buildings, she thinks. Majestic in their filigreed, medieval, gothic collegiate style, but from the water, it's like a diorama— scaled down and curated and fake. On the far side of the Lasalle building, construction of the new dormitories has begun, and a crane is unloading blue Porta Potties onto the grass.

"It looks like a place of worship." Roy says, leaning over the railing and handing her the flask.

"You know how sometimes, when you see something from a distance, you get a sense of its aura?" Joyce says.

"Okay?"

"Nothing at all for me," she says. "I look at RMC, and I feel . . . nothing . . . complete repulsion, actually." She pauses. "Everything is groomed and orderly and stiff and preordained." The whiskey has hit her, and she feels a swirling sense of contentment as she looks at the inscription on the flask: *Bravery is being the only one who knows you're afraid*.

"Three more years," Roy says.

"I don't know, Roy."

"What do you mean?"

"I can't imagine three more years here."

Roy wraps his arm around her shoulder. "Joyce, you need to find your groove. Fire it up."

. . . .

After a full day of sunshine and a few flasks of whiskey, Joyce is lightheaded and buzzed. Back on campus, she walks through the corridors of Lasalle, the tunnel that joins Haldimand, and climbs the stairs to the third floor, the home of Nine Squadron. She searches the brass nameplates on the doors until she finds Fourth-Year Gibbs's room. A Portishead song, "Roads," is playing. She loves that song. She leans her head on his door and knocks.

He is surprised to see her.

"Can I come in?"

"What?"

"I'd like to talk to you."

"Are you drunk?"

His eyes survey her face, which remains neutral. He looks up and down the hallway, then steps aside to let her into his room. As he closes the door, it seems to Joyce that he lowers his shoulders and sucks in his stomach. He notices her glance at the brace on his wrist. "I guess it doesn't really matter at this point," he says.

"Which regiment did you get?" she asks, taking a seat on his bed.

"3 RCR. Afghanistan in January."

"Is that good?"

"I'll be the first in my class to deploy," he says.

Joyce notices an empty can of Pringles on his desk next to a crock of Vaseline Intensive Care lotion.

"I wasn't sure you'd know me," she says.

"You're Roy's best bud, right?" he says. "Joyce?" He sits on his bed next to her. "Roy's a good bagpiper. He's a good guy. You two need to stick together. It's the only way to get through this place."

He is performing, she thinks. Being superior, but she can sense his unease.

"Do you remember when you blindfolded me?"

His eyes become animated and vivid. "Yeah," he says, without any hint of remorse. "I do remember, yeah."

They stare at each other, and Joyce can see the muscles in his jaw. Then, it's as if he recoils and backs down. His gaze lowers and fixes on the floor. "I didn't mean for everyone to crowd around you like that, and the way you fell." He fiddled with the strap on the wrist brace. "I didn't mean . . . can I show you something?" he asks, straightening, taking off his shirt to reveal a shadow of prickly hair-growth on his chest. He shaves his chest, she thinks, taking in his musty scent. He has a good chest, broad and lean. His braced hand fumbles to his shoulder, to the base of a pink scar, drawn and blunt. "I've been making this cut since first year," he says. "It keeps getting longer, and deeper."

Joyce leans in to examine the scar.

"Last summer in Gagetown, it got infected the last week in the field and I almost got my ass medically re-coursed," he says, grimacing. "Almost had to do phase 4 Infantry all over again. No thanks. I stopped, but I think about it. About cutting."

Joyce sits quietly. Gibbs's face is pinched and sad and juvenile. She had expected his surprise at seeing her, but she hadn't prepared for such a confession, and her mind is frantic. A sour scent of fake tanner and sweat, and she leans in closer, touching his scar, tracing it with her finger as it worms its way down the side of his bicep to his elbow. He isn't acting now. He isn't rigid or wilted, and in this moment of neutrality, Joyce registers his torment. She is flooded with it. In this space, she is overcome with a desire to be as close as possible to his suffering. She wants to be memorable to him, to leave an imprint that is equal and greater than the one he has left with her. She is intoxicated by her desire because it is entirely her own. It feels particular and original to her. It's as if his destabilization has opened a space for her. She leans in and kisses his scar. Small, slow, urgent pecks. She lowers her hand to the waistband of his sweatpants where his cock is exposed and erect.

Joyce removes her uniform pants and her panties, and crawls onto him, lowering herself, titling her pelvis. "Slowly," she says, loosening her necktie and unbuttoning her shirt. She holds her breath and lets him enter her gradually. He starts to adjust his position, shifting his hips, but she stops him. "Slowly," she says, "slow," and he responds, leans his forehead into the nape of her neck. When he's inside, she tightens her hold, imagining the thin skin of his cock tunnelling into her. "I don't want to come," she says over the top of his head. "I don't want to come, and I don't want you to come." He looks up at her, closes his eyes, bows his head so that it rests on her chest, and wraps his arms around her.

Joyce returns to her room via the outside quadrangle and courtyard where the flags clang out-of-tune notes on their poles. She can still feel the sensation of him inside her. Gibbs's vulnerability was the opposite of precision, she thinks. The opposite of evenly spaced hangers and deeply polished leather and shirts folded into squares. He is just as lost as she is. For the first time since being here she has feelings of expansiveness. It's something she might be able to work with.

....

On the Sunday before graduation parade, Joyce and Roy attend their final open-mic at The Moth before heading off for summer training — Joyce to Gagetown and Roy to Esquimalt. They settle into a nest of mismatched throw pillows in a corner booth. Burgundy velvet drapes graze the floor, and shelves with leather-bound books and vintage cameras create a cozy, clichéd atmosphere. The small stage glows beneath ceiling spotlights, and beers and cheesecake arrive at their table. Roy is practising his skit, shifting his face between expressions of ecstasy, horror, joy, and exhaustion.

"The Mask Maker," he says, gleefully. "A legendary act, the Mask Maker flips masks on and off his face." Roy makes faces, raising his long fingers in peek-a-boo to switch between each imaginary mask.

"The pathos!" Joyce exclaims.

"But mon amie," Roy continues with drama, "in the end, the Mask Maker puts on a laughing face. A terrific laughing face." Roy raises his hands to his face. When he lowers them, his mouth gapes into a broad, gaudy grin. He bounces about in his seat, luxuriating in the joy of his happy face, but as he tries to remove the laughing mask, it won't come off. The mask is stuck! He lowers his shoulders, bows his head, bangs his fist on the table, descends into despair, all the while maintaining the gaping grin on his face.

"Horrific," Joyce mumbles through a mouthful of cheesecake.

"Awesome, right?!" Roy says. "Here's to second year!" He raises his beer and takes a drink. Joy stares above her at an octopus of a chandelier.

When it's her turn to perform, Joyce walks to the stage, and raises her left arm to catch a hula hoop. She rotates it around her arm, walking rigidly with pointed toes. On the stage, she flicks the hoop straight up in the air and catches it on her neck. Bracing her lower body, she maintains the motion of the hoop, her face a triumphant grin. Her eyes shift and fix on something in the middle distance as another hoop darts in her direction. She moves with quick, short steps to catch it with her head and adjusts the rhythm of her circular motion, extending her arms out front, palms up — *ta-da!* Another hoop is tossed, and she locks it in her gaze, scoops her head to catch it. The hoops are out of sync now, but she keeps them moving with violent circles of her head and neck. They slink to her hips and continue frantic laps of her body. Arms out, palms up — *ta-da!* But there is another hoop, and another, and another, and Joyce's spiralling motion deteriorates into jolted, rigid gestures as the hoops continue to descend upon her. Her arms are no longer presenting, but reaching upward desperately, hooking each new hoop as it wraps and flails around her body. She keeps circling and circling and circling, the motion concentrated in her waist, her feet stepping one-two-one-two-one-two-one-two as the hoops continue their orbit around her core. Finally, abruptly, she lowers both arms, and catches the hoops.

There are no hoops, of course, but Joyce has faith that her audience can see the invisible. She bows. She bows deeply to bountiful applause.

KIJIJI BFF

Elena is sitting on the kitchen floor. Adjacent, the dining room, which will be the playroom, is full of boxes of board games and books, paintbrushes and puzzles, popsicle sticks, scissors, balls of yarn, bottles of glue, tiny plastic dinosaurs. It's four a.m., and crinkled packing paper surrounds her as if she is a fragile item packed inside this kitchen box. Do Not Crush.

To Do:
- internet hookup
- two-way tape
- curtains 168 × 184 cm
- cutlery tray
- toilet brush ×2
- assemble bunk bed
- dryer hookup
- unplug shower drain

Elena's husband and daughters are camping so that she can set up the house at lightspeed. In four days, she unpacks and puts things away. She learns the late-night creaks of the house, the sound of water in the pipes. In the quiet of the wee hours, she imagines the people who lived in this house before her, the content of their cupboards, the stuff of their dreams and desires.

Two boxes overflow with curtains that migrate from house to house, fitting no window twice. Elena doesn't accumulate things in general, but there is always a niggling pressure to repurpose this material; maybe she'll learn to sew as her mother could sew. With every new posting there is opportunity to reinvent.

On Kijiji, an ad for thirty-plus sets of hand-embroidered curtains. *Hi, Jill. Interested in curtains. Can I set up a time to view?*

Jill's small house is engulfed by trees and flowers and shrubs that weave between wind chimes and bird feeders and whirligigs. A bronze statue of a woman holding an urn cascades water into a pond and Elena inhales cedar and humidity as she gets out of her car. In a hammock on the front deck, Jill is reading a catalogue. On the cover, a flawless face with casually rolling eyes and the words, *Glowing Skin Now.*

"It's beautiful here," Elena says.

"Thank you. Elena, right?" Jill is shorter than Elena, but just as pear-shaped. Elena suspects they are close in age — late-thirties. "Coffee?"

Inside, the house opens into a curved wooden ceiling and a panorama of windows that showcase the gardens. A teak sideboard is also curved, its gleaming belly as big as a boat. A glass coffee table has a collection of glass candle holders without candles, and a rawhide rug sprawls before a stone fireplace that exceeds Elena in height. She could walk right into it.

"This space is extraordinary."

"Thank you. It's a James Strutt house," Jill says as she floats around her kitchen.

"From outside, it's so modest."

"That's Strutt," Jill says. "Tiny door opens to an elaborate space. Geometry subverts expectation."

"The ceiling reminds me of a saddle."

"Signature Strutt," Jill says. "Hyperbolic paraboloid. The roof gets its strength from the shape instead of the material." She dumps a spoonful of grinds into the press. "The curvature prevents buckling. Brilliant architect, Strutt."

"You're an architect?"

"Designer. My husband, Massimo, has a landscaping business. Most of the outside work is him, except the pond, that's me."

"This entire space has some kind of a special . . . I don't know—"

Elena thinks about the energy of places all the time, how it can often feel impenetrable to her. Suddenly, tears swell and trickle down her face. "I'm sorry. I, I don't know what's happening," she says, wiping her cheek.

Jill lays a wooden spoon on the counter and walks toward her. "Can I hug you?"

Her scent is sour, but pleasant, like an overripe tomato, and her body is warm. "It's lovely, actually," Jill says, rubbing circles on Elena's back. "Means the world to me. I pour my soul into creating spaces. The layering and scale, the tone of elements."

"We're military, my family," Elena says, collecting herself. "We just moved . . . I wear myself out. I wear myself out every time." She gazes at the ceiling. "Your home is extraordinary."

"Moving is awful," Jill says as she pours coffee. "Just awful. Dismantling and starting over. Ugh." She and her husband used to move a lot with his work, Jill explains. They settled five years ago, and she refuses to move again. "Honestly, I had a life crisis every time we moved."

In a room at the back of the house, curtains hang from the ceiling as if curated. Mostly sheer, some with floral embroidery, others with paisley or geometric patterns.

"Did you embroider these?" Elena asks, examining a pattern of black irises.

"I did."

The curtains sway, brushing against each other in the afternoon light. It's as if they are weeping, Elena thinks as she walks through their labyrinth. Jill is leaning on the doorframe, holding her mug with both hands, a look of concentrated seeing on her face. It's like this stranger is capable of looking right into her, Elena thinks. It's as if Jill understands her in a way that is uncluttered by actually knowing her.

"You have the most beautiful skin, Elena," she says. "Radiant."

The curtains cost more than Elena had budgeted, but she buys a set. With an extendable rod, Jill removes them from their hooks, folds them into perfect squares, wraps them in blue tissue paper, and places them inside a paper bag.

"Would you like to go for a coffee sometime?" Jill asks. "I know what it's like, starting over."

Back in her house, Elena is buzzing with the elation of new friendship. She decides to tackle the silverware she inherited from her mother. She has never used it. Her mother died eleven years ago, and the silverware has clinked around inside its case, nomadic between postings. Inside the case there's a stale, inky smell. One large serving spoon is secured in its proper slot, but the remaining pieces are a nest of tarnished silver. Elena sits on a pile of broken-down boxes to polish each piece. As the silver blooms she thinks of her mother and this generational trend of owning silverware. She thinks of Jill, how she floated through her beautiful home. Jill would appreciate the effort of silverware, Elena thinks, gazing at her upside-down self in the palm of a spoon.

As if summoned, Jill's name illuminates Elena's phone. She is planning to visit some churches that were built by James Strutt, she texts. It's something she's wanted to do for a while. Would Elena like to join her? They could do lunch.

Elena slips a polished knife into its slot. She would like to take shape in this new city. Explore its food, its music and theatre, its thrift shops and green space. Settle in, make good friends, have a sense of direction, become a familiar face. Their last posting was three years in a remote military town north of Toronto. The place had been a wearying enigma to her, and she had responded with aloofness. She hadn't connected with anyone, and it was easy to leave. If she could somehow delete those years, there would be little consequence to anyone. Elena lines up the last pieces of silver in the case — spoons, forks, and knives, keen and orderly as a marching band.

In the living room, standing on a chair, Elena slides the new curtains onto their rod. Sage in colour with black irises on the hem, they are perfect. She removes a toaster oven from the sofa and takes a seat, clicks a photo of the curtains and sends it to Dan. *Love you,* she texts. *Found these curtains on Kijiji! Xox to the girls.* He responds with kissing emojis, hearts for eyes, *Looks great. Love you too. Get some sleep.*

The curtains are creased from having been folded, and she adds a fabric steamer to her list. Jill's warmth and openness this morning made Elena acutely aware of a drought that has crept into her life. It's been years since she's had a close friend. Katie Lamond. She and Katie were pregnant together in Greenwood ten years ago. Emergency c-sections a few days apart, the two of them had been perplexed over the creamy orange surgical glue that oozed from their incisions. Rub a bit of breast milk into those cracked nipples, Katie had said, laughing. Together with their newborns, they'd sat topless in Katie's living room, airing out swollen breasts. Strange new bodies, suppository pain meds, chronic thirst, sleep deprivation. At the time, Elena's grief for her mother was new, and when her daughter was born, the sadness morphed into something vast and imprecise. Time snailed. Lucid, lullaby baby joy coupled with fatigue and discomfort and loss. Katie's friendship was her index, and when they were posted out of Greenwood, when they said their goodbyes, Elena's loneliness ballooned. The skin on her hands and feet peeled raw. No more close friendships, she vowed. Never again.

Elena sinks into the sofa as shadows from the curtains' embroidery project on the wall, darting like fish.

Thanks for the invite, Jill. I'd be happy to join you.

....

The following Sunday, Elena and Jill are exploring the exterior of Trinity United Church. It's just after nine a.m., and a collection of dewy spiderwebs glisten in patches on the lawn.

"An ark of a church," Jill says. "That's what it's been called. An ark of a church."

"No windows?" Elena examines the weathered copper exterior. "It's definitely boat-like. Must be claustrophobic inside with no natural light."

"Wait for it!"

Inside, wooden walls and laminated beams are washed with light from above. A skylight streams diagonal rays into the nave, suspending dust like snow.

"Strutt awakens the senses," Jill gushes, linking arms with Elena as they wander down the aisle. "Honestly, he could make any space sacred."

The church has a sanctuary feel, closed off from the outside world. "But what about cloudy days?" Elena asks. "And at night?"

"Ambient lighting of course," Jill says. "Which reminds me, I *have* to bring you to The Manx. Basement pub downtown, nook seating, dim lighting. It's like a cave."

The next church they visit is the Ethiopian Orthodox Church, which, Jill explains, was St. Peter's Anglican Church when Strutt designed it in 1959. The roof is triangular and extends from its apex to a meter above the ground, making the exterior mostly all roof. Four identical peaks tower with triangular windows.

The roof was made with a spray-on dry-mix concrete slurry to create a series of steep peaks and deep valleys. Jill narrates from her phone. *This concrete slurry could assume any shape once it was applied to the framework with high-pressure hoses.*

To Elena, the exterior is gloomy. The dips and peaks feel dense and tedious, like something collapsing. Inside, the folds of the roof create arches pierced by windows — a spectacular effect, but she wonders at the uninviting exteriors. How could the architect be so sure there would be enough curiosity to draw people inside? It feels disingenuous. Her interest wanes, and she's happy when Jill suggests they go for lunch.

Jill takes her to a restaurant called Whalebone, and they order white wine and a platter of smoked fish to share.

"Cheers to new friends and mid-century architecture!" Jill says brightly, raising her glass. "By the way, your skin is glowing. What is your secret?"

"Oiliness," Elena says, smiling. "An excess of oil and a lack of sleep."

Over lunch, Elena and Jill discuss husbands, kids, work, in-laws, skincare routines. Jill just finished an extensive kitchen renovation for a client and is taking the summer off. Elena hasn't worked full-time as a nurse since the kids were born. Jill bought a canoe on Kijiji for seventy-five dollars. Elena went on a canoe trip with Dan when they lived in Cold Lake, Alberta.

"So, you must have a network of friends all over," Jill says, folding a sliver of smoked salmon onto a piece of bread.

"I guess," Elena says. She tells Jill about the time Dan was deployed to Afghanistan and a group of military wives invited her to watch *The Bachelor* on Tuesday nights. There is a sort of barrenness to these friendly circles, Elena explains. Everyone would be moving on in a year or two and the friendships respond to that.

"It's not that the women are shallow or incapable of intimacy," Elena says. "They are just adapting to a sort of chronic transience."

"You can never predict how your life will morph," Jill says. "Military wives remind me of Strutt's concrete slurry," she says between bites. "The way it takes on any shape."

The bill arrives and Elena pays for the meal. "My treat. Thanks for inviting me."

At home that night, Elena folds laundry while Dan sits on their bedroom floor assembling a bookshelf.

"Jill is really great," she tells Dan. "She's sweet and welcoming and kind of tacky. I like her." Elena secures a stack of towels under her chin and carries them to the bathroom. "She wants to visit more Strutt architecture — that Ottawa architect who built her house. I'm kind of over him. He's like a trickster. It's obnoxious."

"You should go," Dan says. "It's good for you to meet people this early in the posting."

. . . .

The following Friday, Elena drives up a winding driveway located in a densely forested suburb. Jill is on the front step scrolling on her phone.

"Welcome to the maple tree house," she says as Elena gets out of her car. "Built for the Bormann family by James Strutt in 1965. The current owners are friends of mine." Jill dangles a set of keys. "Ana and Rick are in Alaska for three weeks. I water the plants."

Inside, the bungalow opens to an angular wooden ceiling studded with skylights that funnel around a giant maple tree. "The house is built around the tree," Jill explains, "like a scattered deck of cards." Jill wanders casually, sliding her fingers along a bulky sideboard. A giant buffalo head with glossy nostrils is mounted on a brick wall above a fireplace.

"What I love about this house are the angles," Jill says. "So many angles. It's like being inside a kaleidoscope." She opens the sideboard and grabs a bottle of Hennessy. "Brandy?"

They roam through the dining room, which is furnished with a glass oval table and wooden chairs. A pot of white orchids is the table's centrepiece, and a gnarly wooden pedestal with swirls of knots provides a central, underneath sort of intelligence. It's hard to imagine that people live here, Elena thinks, noticing the absence of disarray — no shoes or stacks of mail or recyclables. Like at Jill's house, a panorama of windows overlooks a forested exterior. As they walk through a winding hallway of wood-panelled walls and terracotta tile floors, Elena stops to look at a painting.

"Les Automatistes. Of this I am sure, mademoiselle," Jill says in mock Quebecois. "I bet it's Riopelle. My dad has a Riopelle in his office." The painting seems to have been created with blades.

"Do they have kids?"

"God no."

In the master bedroom, Jill sets down her drink and flops onto the bed. "You can see the maple tree from every room," she says, pointing her toe toward a glass opening near the ceiling.

Back in the living room, Jill pours herself another drink and fills Elena's glass. She takes the bottle with her to the back of the house, where a staircase descends to an outdoor pool. The sun is setting.

Jill slips out of her dress and kicks off her panties. Her pubic hair, a tidy oval, is like a peephole, and the skin on her ass is slack and dimpled. She dives into the pool.

Elena unbuttons her blouse, removes her bra, her long floral skirt and panties, and steps slowly into the pool, which is shaped like a kidney bean. The water is warmer than the air.

"You are seriously game for anything," Jill says as Elena wades into the water. "I just love you."

"Not anything, exactly," Elena replies, "but this isn't terrible."

Jill smiles as she floats on her back, staring at the sky.

"Are you sure they won't mind?" Elena asks.

"Ana is like a sister. You'll meet her soon. She and Rick own a restaurant in Little Italy. I'll take you," Jill says. "You just missed one of their epic parties, actually. Everyone wore animal print. A few of the husbands broke out leopard-print leggings. Giant blow-up zebras and giraffes and crocodiles everywhere. Rick wore a Tilley with khaki shorts and vest and a badge that said *Cougar Hunter,*" she says laughing. "I lost my earring in the pool that night, one of my favourite earrings."

Elena can't remember the last time she attended a social event that wasn't organized by the military family resource centre. A spaghetti dinner, a trivia night, something annual and regimented. Her mother used to host parties in their house. Fellow teachers, rye and ginger, bean salad. Jill climbs out of the pool and pours another drink.

From the water, Elena gazes at the rose gold sky. The brandy has hit her and a smooth heaviness floods the space behind her eyes. She feels completely out of touch, but is familiar with this emotion — this deep disconnect. She thinks of Jill's hug on the day they met, how it had outlined the extent of her detachment.

Something darts above her. "A bat! Look!" she yells.

On the pool deck, Jill wails, drops the bottle of brandy, smacks at the air around her, spills her drink, and steps on broken glass. "Fuck!"

Elena gets out of the pool and rushes to Jill, who has fallen into a lounger and is cradling her bleeding foot. The dark folds of her labia gape open like a wrinkled, screaming mouth.

Elena squats and takes Jill's foot in her hand. "Lie back," she says. "Try to breathe deeply."

As Elena removes slivers of glass from the sole of Jill's foot, she thinks about the time she and Dan discovered a small bat colony in their attic. It was years ago; they were posted to Winnipeg. Bats had soared around their kitchen and living room. One tucked itself between the pane and screen of their bedroom window. Its little monkey face. Translucent wings folded around itself like an umbrella.

"They eat insects," Elena says.

"They're fucking creepy."

Elena lowers Jill's foot. "Polysporin before bed tonight."

The night air has cooled, and when Elena dives back into the pool, the water is thermal.

"I love how fuckin' calm you are," Jill says, lowering herself into the pool. "Like, just try to breathe deeply, like, seriously, nothing fazes you." She swims toward Elena and their legs touch. "I'm so happy we met. I've wanted to meet someone like you for ages." Jill leans her head back, submerging her face to her jawline. "Do you find," she says dreamily, "the universe just like, opens sometimes?"

"Sometimes," Elena says as their arms link. "Mostly I notice how quickly things can change. I try not to set my heart on anything." She cringes at this burst of self-pity, but Jill doesn't seem to notice. Jill is tranquil, her eyes and mouth closed as if she's humming something classical.

It's past midnight when the two emerge from the pool. As they dry off, Elena suggests that Jill call her husband for a ride home since she's had a lot to drink. Jill insists she is fine. It's been hours.

From her bed, Elena texts Jill. *Tonight was magical. Thank you again. Text when you're home.*

Jill seems too good to be true, she thinks as she spoons into Dan. It makes her weary, causes her usual rigid self to dabble in possibility. She drifts into sleep and dreams: glass shards and compressed metal and the bloody sole of Jill's foot, and then her mother appears, bald, gaunt, pointing at the scars of her double mastectomy. "It's not so bad," she says in earnest. "The surgeon did a marvellous job. I'd be more upset if I'd lost a tooth." A car has ploughed into the trunk of a maple tree, its headlights blinding. Wilting house-plants and shattered glass candleholders on the pool deck and Jill's face is uncurious: "I'll take care of it," she slurs, her naked body glinting metallic. With a broom she sweeps glass into the pool and as the fragments descend, the aquamarine water darkens to grey. Elena is wandering inside the house, past the painting made with blades, past the glossy buffalo nostrils. Through the skylights, the maple tree is animated and making faces.

Her phone wakes her. A text from Jill. *It was a super special night. Soooo glad we met. See you soon. Xox Jill*

. . . .

49

The following Friday, Elena and Jill meet at Il Primo, Ana and Rick's restaurant in Little Italy. When Elena arrives, Jill is already there and has ordered a bottle of red and a charcuterie board.

Rick arrives with ice water. "Ana is enroute," he says to Jill as he fills her glass. "You've had a stellar month, I hear."

"Rick, this is Elena," Jill says sharply. "We met on Kijiji."

"The military spouse!" he says, smiling. "Boss! Military wives. Holy global network. Welcome to the Alitone team, Elena." He fills Elena's glass before moving on to another table.

Jill's eyes widen, and she adjusts the neckline of her dress. "Have you ever thought of selling skincare products, Elena?"

"What?" Elena says, baffled. "No. No, never."

"You should think about it," Jill says, swirling her wine. "Our skincare company is called Alitone. Easy money. Flex schedule. Portable. It's perfect for someone like you who moves so often. I would love it if you joined our team." Jill stands abruptly. "Ana!" Tall and elegant, Ana is wearing a green linen dress with scoop pockets. A chunky silver link bracelet dangles from her wrist. "Ana, meet Elena."

"Great to meet you, Elena. I'm Jill's team leader. Jill has been raving about you." Ana glances at Jill. "And lady, you are right—flawless skin."

Elena can feel Jill's eyes on her. There's something new in her composure. Something tense and impatient and depraved. Ana removes an iPad and sample products from her bag.

"I noticed it the very first time we met," Jill says to Ana. "The skin brightener would practically sell itself." Jill takes Elena's hand. "You are going to be amazing."

"Um, how was Alaska?" Elena asks awkwardly as Ana takes a seat.

"Out of this world." Ana sips her wine as she scrolls on her tablet. "Jill gave you the tour of the house? Did she mention it's shaped like a scattered deck of cards? Isn't that incredible? Team members are welcome to use the house when they need a space to promote the product, or if they want a relaxing venue to get to know a potential new client." Ana piles slices of prosciutto on a piece of bread and opens her mouth so wide, Elena can see the silver fillings of her molars.

....

At home, Dan is in bed, snoring. Elena makes chamomile tea, draws the curtains closed. Earlier, after everyone had left the restaurant, she sat in her car, staring at herself as a tiny blue dot blinking amidst a maze of streets, polygon green spaces, square houses. Blue dot blinking. No bearings to speak of.

On the sofa, she sips her tea. She is in touch with this disappointment, her default sorrow — there it is, oh faithful friend. She yearns for her mother.

She sends a text: *Thanks for tonight, Jill. Ana is great.*

Maybe she could sell skincare products, Elena thinks. She'd meet people, join a community, go to pool parties. Maybe it could become her thing.

Ana adored you. I knew she would. Soooo?

The curtains are still creased from when Jill folded them into squares. In the absence of light, they look like cement. A wall made with dull, grey cement blocks.

I don't think Alitone is for me, Jill. I'm sorry.

Minutes pass.

Thanks for considering me though. I hope we can still hang out. I've really enjoyed spending time together.

Radio silence.

Elena goes upstairs, gets dressed for bed, washes her face. As she is brushing her teeth, her phone lights up.

That's unfortunate. It was great to meet you. Enjoy your time in the area.

Elena continues brushing her teeth with one hand while scrolling through her phone with the other. She scrolls and scrolls and scrolls. She opens her to-do list and touches the fabric steamer. Delete.

Delete items? You cannot undo this action.

She leans over and spits in the sink.

Delete.

ART OF CAMOUFLAGE

It was week four of a twelve-week artillery course at the combat training centre in Gagetown. Diesel fumes seeped into the canvas-covered vehicle where they sat side by side like eggs in a carton. Rifles stood upright between legs, helmets leaned on muzzles, eyes closed to avoid dust or to steal a nap before the sun came up. Brown, black, and green camouflage paint concealed necks and faces. Ellie had not yet mastered the art of camouflage, texturing the paint in such a way as to appear one with her surroundings. She was mostly green.

"Coates, you look like Kermit," said Brad Fury, glancing around, willing others to laugh with him. Lean and bold, he looked down at Ellie and smirked. He looked down on everyone. A young man guided by principles of war, he fortified himself with weaker allies, overtaking others like a black creeping mildew. He took up more space than he needed.

Ellie dreaded days on the rifle range, on the ground in prone position with the smell of oil and metal and parched dirt coating her throat and skin. Her eyes pressed shut as she squeezed the trigger. From the beginning, she wished it would end. Breathe, hold, fire. Assume a natural alignment. Relax facial muscles. Breathe, hold, fire. Follow through. She pulled the trigger and waited for the rifle to fire, the recoil rattling her every time. Was this make-believe? Was she really lying on the ground firing bullets at targets? She looked at the others in her row, on stomachs, aligning sites, relaxing facial muscles. Her bullet groupings were like a scattered spread of anthills.

"Guess that's why the Newfies love hunting moose," Brad taunted, rubbing shoulders with his elf-like sidekick, Oliver Lee. Oliver shared none of Brad's swagger but most of his shadow. Brad mocked him constantly, mostly over his failures with women, but Oliver seemed to enjoy the attention. She guessed he preferred mockery to obscurity. Ellie absorbed Brad's Newfie jokes as any good Newfoundlander was conditioned to do. Laughed it off — chuckled even. Resentment's party dress is a good hearty chuckle.

Later that week, during a field march, weighted down with an ill-fitted rucksack, Ellie stared at the heels of the person ahead of her for twelve kilometres. Back and neck aching, feet blistered, she shuffled to keep in file. Combat boots wrecked her feet, and by the end of the week her heels were raw, and her body was bruised in all the delicate places.

Eager to escape the confines of the military base, on the weekend Ellie rode her bicycle for over an hour to the city of Fredericton. There, she wandered the mall with a farmer's tan, green with envy of the highly groomed barista, Ella, at Second Cup coffee shop, and of her friends who loitered. Their nails, short and painted dark pinks and blues. Laces of sandals crept up polished, unbruised legs. Eyelids sparkled; eyelashes flared like cartoon cat eyes. Ellie and the barista were nearly the same age — early twenties — separated by only a few vowels. Ellie sat cross-legged to conceal her bruised legs and her heels that leaked puss and blood. She stayed there for hours doing her homework, studying the girls and their hierarchies alongside the principals of leadership in field artillery, where, unless otherwise noted, masculine pronouns applied to both men and women. The girls enjoyed free lattes and planned their summer evenings of fires on the beach or coolers on the deck. One of the girls was making jewelry from seashells. She wore rings on most of her fingers.

"Beautiful rings," Ellie said to the girl.

"Thank you. Try one." The girl was gentle and smelled of honey and rosewater.

Ellie tried one on. The skin on her hands was full of cuts and dirt. Her nails gritty even though she had scrubbed them with a brush. The girl's hands were sinewy and artfully adorned with seashells.

"You garden, don't you?" the girl asked, smiling.

"Oh, no." Ellie hesitated. "I'm in the army . . . at the school I mean. In Gagetown."

"Oh. Wow!" The girl's enthusiasm embarrassed Ellie. "I'm saving for my student exchange to Barcelona. Going in September."

Ellie bought three shell rings. They were sharp and cut into her hands, but she liked them. At closing time, she biked the dark highway back to the base. A car blared its horn as it passed, and a guy yelled out his window.

"What the fuck, girl?"

Exactly, she thought.

. . . .

The following weekend, Ellie decided to check in with the guys on the course about a study group. As she walked down the hallway, she heard a group of them in Brad's room laughing and one of them yelling 'holy shit.' Brad, Oliver and three others hovered over a laptop watching a video.

"Ellie, watch this. It's fucking awesome," Brad yelled. The guys cowered as she approached, and somehow she knew they were celebrating something vile. The video showed a woman sucking a horse's penis before it ejaculated all over her face. The guys howled.

"Jesus." Ellie felt her face heat.

"Ellie, it's just a joke. Don't be like that," Brad said as she walked away. "It's not like anyone forced her to do it. It was her choice." He was triumphant. She pictured him putting salt on the belly of a frog and watching the frog explode, guts and skin and tiny eyeballs splattering everywhere. Brad would do that, she thought. He'd attack an opponent at their critical vulnerability. Suppress, harass, destroy.

Ellie left the base and biked to the local marina where she claimed a picnic table near the water. She watched a group of people climb on board a boat and slowly motor away. Their wake formed an arrowhead in the water, indicating their direction, their purpose. This way to the good life. The wake reminded her of arcs of fire. The invisible slice that is the scope of a weapon's reach, the range and breadth of its killing potential. Those arcs that must overlap with other friendly fire to shatter enemy moral and physical cohesion. The man-oeuvrist approach to warfare. Sheltered by dense green trees, the marina smelled of moss and mould and damp wood, and Ellie wished she could learn to manoeuvre a boat onto the lake. She wished it didn't compel her to think of kill zones. After sunset, she biked back to her barracks on the base. Four beds in her room, no roommates, pale green walls. The only sounds were the birds and the occasional thunder of a leopard tank rumbling back to base after a field exercise.

Later in the night, guys from the course stumbled in from the bars. She heard Brad yell something about moose meat before he banged on her door. "Ellie, you there? Ellie? C'mon

Ellie." He rattled her doorknob. "Ellie, open up." She felt the urge to punch him in the face. He's drunk, she thought, he'd never expect it. Element of surprise. Ambush. She quietly walked to her closet and slipped her new seashell rings on her fingers, picturing Brad with a scabbed, bruised eye, tenderly applying camouflage paint to his face the following week in the field, sweat and dirt infecting his wound, making it throb and drool. In her nightgown, her hand on the doorknob, she listened as he continued to pound and kick. "Open the fucking door, Ellie," impatient, as if she was somehow wasting his precious time.

She'd punch him hard with her right hand. Her bare legs shook.

"Fuck it." He walked away, thwarted. Ellie stared at the door until her legs stopped shaking. Her right hand still clenched in a fist; the shells cutting her skin and spilling tiny droplets of blood on the floor.

. . . .

A few days later their leadership skills were tested with a week of eight-hour tasks. Each student had a turn locating and setting up a position for the deployment of a six-gun battery. Ellie received her orders, plotted her route, and made a quick time appreciation. Getting there was the hardest part. The armoured vehicles trained in the same area, turning the ground into a web of transient trails.

"Don't trust the trails," her instructor, Captain Riggs, warned. "Get your bearings immediately and focus on the larger navigational picture. Tree lines, depressions, scrub, stream junctions, hilltops."

But it was all unfamiliar terrain to Ellie. It was dense brush, sand, tank ruts, marshes, mosquitoes, and a troop of soldiers who wanted nothing more than a quick set-up with time to spare before the gun battery arrived, for a cigarette and a bag of chips and a can of Pepsi.

Following a series of miscalculations, ill-fated orientation and indecision, she set up a gun position in haste, planting six gun-markers in the required 'w' formation. The angles were correct. The guns could be positioned as to avoid firing over each other or into a treeline. Her kill zones overlapped perfectly. But the ground was as soft as a loaf of bread. An unmarked marshy area. Captain Riggs stood near her, taking notes. She waited on the side of the road, soaked above her knees, listening for the rumble of the guns.

The six trucks arrived, each carrying a gun detachment of eight soldiers and towing a 105 mm howitzer. She directed them to their positions. The trucks hobbled and sunk as they plunged off the road into the swamp where she had set the markers. The following two hours were spent digging, towing, and swearing until all trucks and guns were back on solid ground, dripping with mud and moss. Ellie walked around, face green, helmet lopsided. She offered help, but mainly stayed out of the way. People avoided eye contact.

"Officer Cadet Coates, you're done. Command post for debrief."

Ineffective leadership, ineffective time management, ineffective situational awareness. Fail. Retest required.

For the rest of the week in the field, Ellie participated in her course mates' assessments.

"Coates, you're on survey," they said. The easiest, most foolproof job was survey. They didn't take their chances. She watched her peers make executive decisions well enough to receive a passing grade while she held the survey instrument like a dunce. With each step, her feet burned inside her combat boots, wool socks scrubbing her open blisters. She reeked of DEET and sweat. The height of luxury was removing her boots, brushing her teeth, and wiping her face with a wet cloth before settling on the ground for two or three hours of sleep. Too exhausted to set up a shelter, she crawled into her sleeping bag and stared at the stars.

Ellie's grandmother had raised eleven children without electricity or a husband, because Grandfather was often in the mines or on the drink. She wore a working dress and an apron, wound her hair up in a bun, baked her daily bread, and said the rosary on her walk to the well. No nonsense. She didn't hesitate or second guess or regret her insults or her decisions or her methods. She didn't waste time; she didn't waste anything. When asked about the leaner times, she said it never occurred to her to throw her hands up in the air and cry. She had mouths to feed. One day, at her grandmother's house, Ellie, noticing her reflection in a window, straightened up, sucked in her stomach, and placed her hand on her midriff. "Stop lookin' at yourself, child," her grandmother scolded from the kitchen where she stirred a pot of stew. Simmering.

Grandmother endured. She submitted in an orderly fashion to the context of her time. Was this urge to endure woven neatly into Ellie's genes, keeping her here on the ground sleeping under the stars?

Ellie's retest started at ten p.m. on the last day. She had to deploy the guns by zero six hundred hours. Rain pelted her face and darkness made her dizzy. Her course mates were tired, wet, and anxious for the weekend.

"Oliver likes 'em old." Jeering, Brad gave Oliver a shove. "She was at least forty. Took her high heels off and dragged Ollie out of the bar. He was so drunk with his thumbs up. Tits fallin' out of her shirt."

Ellie looked down as she walked past, holding her breath as if avoiding his poison.

With a forty-pound theodolite compass in each hand, rifle slung over her shoulder, she made her way to a mound to set up. Her boot sank into a muddy tank rut, and she tumbled, face first, into a ditch of oily water. For the next seven-and-a-half hours, sweat and water dripped from her face onto her notepad, which was a mess of numbers and angles and fire orders. Her orders into the radio were hesitant and muffled. She repeatedly held the receiver to her chest to afford herself a moment to breathe and swallow and keep the tears at bay. She wanted to weep, but crying would be the end. Crying would be an act of surrender.

It amazed Ellie, the way it came together that morning. The six trucks arrived, guns in tow, and deployed onto her gun position in an orderly fashion. Later, from the command post, she delivered the fire orders to the guns on her position. It was the anticipated final fire mission before returning to base, when all remaining ammunition would be expended. Over the radio, she heard the forward observer's call for fire:

"ZULU-TANGO TWO-ONE-FOUR-SIX, E BATTERY, ADJUST FIRE."

She got to work, calculating and plotting data for the guns, the safety officer peering over her back. Ellie considered the rotation of the earth in her calculations and pictured the craters she was about to make in it. Bus-sized craters.

"FIRE MISSION BATTERY. ADJUSTING ZULU-TANGO TWO-ONE-FOUR-SIX," her voice wailed over the loudspeaker. It sounded lightweight, not serious enough to be ordering the projection of heavy explosives down range. Nonetheless, each detachment commander repeated her order back to her. She glanced out the portal window of the command post. Like ants, the soldiers raced to their positions at the guns, bracing to move them if necessary. Other soldiers prepared the ammunition, checked fuses, or leaned over the sites and the scales, awaiting further orders, eagerly awaiting their angles. It was a race to be the first gun detachment ready to fire.

"H.E. QUICK CHARGE FOUR. PREPARE TWELVE ROUNDS PER GUN. BEARING NUMBER ONE: FOUR-TWO-FIFE-EIGHT, NUMBER TWO: FOUR-TWO-FIFE-ONE, NUMBER THREE: FOUR-TWO-FOUR-EIGHT. . ." She heard the commotion on the gun position as her voice boomed over all of it.

"LOAD." More yells. Breaches slammed shut.

"AT MY COMMAND. ELEVATION NUMBER ONE: FOUR-ONE-SIX, NUMBER TWO: FOUR-TWO-EIGHT, NUMBER THREE: FOUR-TWO-SIX. . ." she continued to deliver the fire orders that would send thousands of pounds of heavy explosives eight kilometres down range. It occurred to her that she had learned a language. She thought of being in Barcelona and speaking in fire orders.

"NUMBER FOUR, READY!" Number four gun was always the fastest.

"NUMBER THREE, READY!"

"NUMBER SIX, READY!"

"NUMBER FIFE, READY!"

"NUMBER TWO, READY!"

"NUMBER ONE, READY!"

The soldiers held the fire lanyards in their hands.

Ellie looked out at the guns as she gave the order to fire: "TWELVE ROUNDS FIRE FOR EFFECT. FIRE!"

"FIRE!" The detachment commanders yelled, almost synchronized, and the guns fired. Deafening blasts. Ellie watched the howitzers recoil as rounds exploded out of muzzles, leaking fumes of propellant and smoke and the ascetic smell of sulphur in a lingering haze.

"Go, go, go!" Loaders hustled to get the next round of ammunition in the barrel, lifting with their legs. Sites checked, scales balanced, yells of "ON" and "READY" and "FIRE!" Hands to ears.

Ellie remembered her first summer of training on the gun position two years ago. When the gun fired, there was a loud crack inside her left ear. The blast of the gun persisted over the ringing in her ear. A shrill, unwavering tone continued inside her head for almost three months. Later, she'd struggle to have conversations in crowded places. 'Can't mess with a classic' would sound like 'that mess was fantastic.' The gun's mark on her inner ear, a minute, deafening crater.

. . . .

On the weekend following the eight-hour tasks, Ellie called her father to tell him she was quitting. She was miserable, she said. She had written her memo.

"Ellie, honey, with only five weeks left?"

But five weeks was an eternity. She went for a run and imagined life outside the military. She'd start with a job in a coffee shop. Maybe she'd travel Europe and learn to speak romance languages. Her bruises would fade. Her chafed body would recover and become smooth and supple. She would paint her nails and let her hair down and breathe freely. She'd have conversations about bridges and birds and mustard seed. She would blossom, unencumbered.

Mail arrived. A yellow envelope with her father's signature scrawl. The contents void of note or letter, just a hardcover picture book, *The Tortoise and the Hare*. Ellie changed tack and floundered through to the end of the course. As if on cue, Brad broke his femur during the final exercise and was medically re-coursed to the winter serial of training. During the graduation parade, Ellie dissected the speeches about future leaders and peacekeepers and her country's role, searching for resonance, for a sense of accomplishment that must be intrinsic to such ceremonies. But it was fruitless. She was on a stage, in a costume, make-believing. Try as she might, she could not make herself believe. Among the spectators, Brad stood with crutches during the national anthem. People patted his back and shook his hand and wished him luck. He had tripped over his own foot and broken his own bone, yet acknowledgement of his success was unquestioned. His achievement was secured, postponed to a later date. The future was his.

. . . .

Years later, when Ellie's children were born, she was introduced to the concept of 'failure to thrive,' when a child failed to attain expected weight percentiles. As a mother, if something didn't work, she abandoned her strategy and tried something new. After twenty years in the military, Ellie finally found the courage to abandon it. She still told lies. When asked, she said she cherished the unique experiences. She reminisced that her time in the military taught her valuable life lessons. Depending on her audience, sometimes she even said she missed it, missed the structure, the uniform, the uniformity.

She crossed paths with Brad once. He had a high rank and a slim wife and two young daughters. He had filled out, was congenial, gracious. He hugged Ellie and introduced her as an old army friend, and Ellie wondered if he could possibly have been as bad as she remembered. Or had she been the player? Toying in a world where she didn't belong. The conversation morphed into life being short and kids growing fast and water under the bridge and the importance of knowing when to quit.

And she couldn't help but wonder, was he pretending now, or had he been pretending then? And she smiled a lot and showed something like mercy.

PANGAEA FRAGMENTED

The mother peels continents from plastic that smells like gasoline. A map of the world pulled from its cardboard tube is determined to curl in on itself. Africa rolls into Australia rolls into Europe and Asia, making a continental sandwich with Finland slipping out the side like a pickle. Plastic nations merge into the giant supercontinent of Pangaea.

The mother could use a second person to hold down the other side of the world map, but the husband and three children have left. Perhaps they will visit a museum with dinosaur bones. Perhaps they will hike to the caves. The mother does not know how they will spend their day, but she is relieved that they have left. She can sense a loosening, as though she might blend into the grain of the manufactured wood floor beneath her. After they left, she wiped the countertop with broad, slow sweeps, marvelling at the surface spirals.

You may consider joining a choir to luxuriate in harmonious frequencies. Are you able to recall your earliest symptoms of depersonalization?

A pile of family photobooks collects dust on the coffee table. The mother positions the books on the corners of the world map that is now spread across the floor. The 2010 photobook sits on a part of Russia that resembles a turkey's head, the snood hanging. The mother read *Days of Terror* when she was twelve and learned about Bolsheviks and precarity. At the time, the scariest part of the book was when bandits entered a home, and the family served them soup as a winter storm rattled panes. She recalls the book as a sequence of grey and rust-coloured images; dainty plates leaning on thin brass stands.

On the cover of the 2010 photobook, the husband swings the son, Colum, over the sea. Colum was four years old that summer. The husband is knee deep in water and he flies the child at eye level so that in the picture, Colum's body is parallel with the horizon. The mother is skilled at capturing moments that involve geometry and gravity. It is unfortunate though, that the expression on Colum's face is hidden, and she imagines his pink shiny cheekbones of unfiltered joy. When little, during times of exhilaration, Colum would grab his penis and say that it tingled. The mother links into that thrilling moment of deeply coded elation.

But now, a swell of sorrow. Her rage from earlier is still within her — not rage anymore, but its stain — from when she grabbed Colum's arm, leaving indentations with her nails. Four tiny crescent moon slivers. The skin around it will most certainly turn blue. "Get your fucking hands off me," he had said to her as he whipped his arm free, scowling. He would have felt the sting of her claw for some time, the rush of blood cells swarming to repair the damage she had inflicted.

I'm curious about your thoughts on enmeshment. Are you able to differentiate your sense of self, your identity, from your surroundings, for example?

This morning, Colum, now fourteen, left the bathroom door open while he urinated on the toilet seat. On the floor, glossy yellow puddles. The mother had spent the morning shuffling around the house like a facsimile of herself, torqued as she collected moldy apple cores, dehydrated orange peels, popcorn and pretzels, soiled socks and underwear, hard, half-eaten cheese slices, chip bags, and aluminum foil compressed into tight, polychromatic balls. The mother fell apart, morphed into something savage, said useless and disgusting, felt the propulsion of something ugly and said piece of shit. Colum's jaw was rigid as he filled the toilet bowl with lemon-scented disinfectant wipes, and when it overflowed, the mother waded barefoot through the sludge, grabbed his arm, and flung him.

"Get your fucking hands off me."

The husband piled the three kids into the van and left the mother wiping countertops with vigour, contemplating her sense of self. Mother. Wife. Savage. She scored a diamond shape into the skin of a pear to remove a small bruise that had quietly tunnelled its way to the fruit's slippery core.

Perhaps a tea. On the wall below the kitchen cupboard, the coffee tin and the jar of honey make a shadow that takes the form of a ship. A polygon of a vessel sailing, the lines and shades and angles as concrete as concrete. The house is still and quiet after so much commotion, and the mother is enchanted by the hum of leaves outside the kitchen window, how they paw at the breeze.

Alfred Wegener was a German polar researcher and record-setting balloonist who noticed the jigsaw puzzle of the Americas and Africa and Europe, the complimentary coastlines of Antarctica and Australia. On the map of the world, the mother finds the beach from the 2010 photobook — a pincer-shaped cove on the northeastern coast of Newfoundland's Avalon Peninsula. That day on the beach there was a wedding between two handsome men. The mother places her finger inside the pincer-shaped cove.

....

They walked to the east side of the beach so as not to intrude on the wedding ceremony. The baby was strapped marsupial to the mother's front, the two-year-old was perched on the father's shoulders, and four-year-old Colum ran beside them, dodging small frothy waves that pearled lace patterns on the sand. They passed families and picnics. A man spoke on his phone while throwing a stick for a German Shepherd dog that barrelled through the water. "An air conditioner," the man said as they passed. "An air conditioner fell to the street below." He threw the stick. "Christ. From the eighteenth floor. Jesus."

On either side of the beach, looming cliffs pressed into the sea. The mother spread her blanket on the rocks, resisting thoughts of the German Shepherd gnawing her baby's face into a meaty pulp.

Small acts of bravery can often be an effective strategy to counter such conjurings. A walk along the beach during which time you might have befriended the dog, for example.

Fingers of metamorphic rock reached into the water on the mother's side of the beach, and the low tide revealed kelp that glinted in the sun. Wegener believed that Pangaea fragmented, vast turbulent forces within the Earth's mantle drifted continents over long periods of geological time. Wegener's character was ridiculed and maligned with claims that he distorted the continents to make them fit.

As the husband flew Colum parallel to the horizon, the mother seized her camera, took a knee, and captured the moment. The baby started to cry, so the mother settled cross-legged on the blanket to nurse.

Since the rogue wave of 1984, locals avoided this beach. The wave engulfed the coast and swept up the hill to the far side of the parking lot, dragging thirty-six people into the sea, three of whom were drowned. Despite this menace, the mother felt secure on this beach; since childhood, it had been her truest sanctuary. The whorl and gyre of air and sea braided her into past generations. So dwarfed, she felt nestled inside overlapping layers of lifetimes.

The mother counted eighteen wedding guests. Trekking barefoot across the beach rocks, the handsome men waded into the waves holding hands. On a high table, two doves perched inside a cage draped in white tulle that surrendered in the breeze. Other guests watched from inside their cordon of asymmetrically strung lights. The mother imagined the well-dressed guests escaping frantically up the hill, beach rocks giving way beneath their bare feet, the birdcage bobbing on a slant in the swell of the sea.

And how long did these thoughts continue? Did you recognize that they were conjured?

The mother's gaze returned to the baby still attached to her breast, sleeping soundly, suckling every so often like an intermittent pulse. Further down the beach, the husband dipped the two-year-old's toes into the frigid water, kissing her neck when her chubby thighs recoiled. The husband lived inside every moment. A super-dad, he rarely obsessed over anything. "Just take breaks when you need them." The husband is classic and patient as steel.

Clouds shifted over the sun, and a darkness surrounded the mother on her blanket, as though she had entered a dim room on a bright day. The baby's eyes opened, and her mini fist padded the mother's breast. A slight shift of the mother's nipple on the roof of the baby's mouth as she continued her rhythmic sucking. The flow of milk like thin threads tugging, and the mother imagined that the threads were golden. It was during such golden moments that she felt the equal or greater pull of dread. She could not shake the feeling — it was more like a fog than a form, and it sustained a wretchedness within her. A weight of despair. She could not breathe it away.

Can you describe it in greater detail, this inner vacuum and how it might connect to your feelings of detachment from your children?

Where was Colum?

He was nowhere.

He had disappeared.

As the mother scanned the length of the beach for Colum, a stick flew midair, and the German Shepherd plunged into the sea. On the other side of the beach, the wedding ceremony was a blur. The husband could be seen in the blur with the two-year-old on his shoulders like a totem. He conversed with guests while drinking a beer. A winning personality, the husband blended seamlessly into any social terrain.

On her side of the beach, the mother peered at the rocks that fingered out into the sea. There was Colum. A tiny silhouette. A crouched figure on all fours. Squirrel-limber, he manoeuvred the slippery surface as water whirled deep and black below him.

Had he come across a fossil out there on the rocks? Wegener used fossils to support his theory of continental drift. Was Colum staring at an ammonoid with its coiled, ornamented shell? In her peripheral, the mother spied the German Shepherd, a Jack-in-the-box begging for another round of fetch, but the man, deeply immersed in his phone, paid the dog no heed.

The baby did not cry when the mother detached her from her breast, tightened the cocoon swaddle, and placed her on the blanket between the cooler and Colum's Spider-Man lifejacket. She moved quickly toward the rocky point, where Colum continued to crouch intently. Maybe he'd found a small pool where previous waves of high tide deposited starfish or snails. He enjoyed plucking snails from the rocks and watching them retreat inside the tiny trapdoors of their shells.

. . . .

When the soles of her feet touched the water, a cold ache shot up the mother's spine, shivering her scalp. An electricity behind her eyes and then the mewling bawl of the baby. Above, high upon the cliffs, louder noises. Engine noises. The mother watched, astounded, as a Dodge Ram truck flew off the cliff. Whirr of tires. It nosedived and tumbled, ricocheting rocks and sand, then hissed and steamed as it sunk below the water. The husband with the two-year-old in his arms ran toward the mother, past the man on his phone, who was jubilant, jumping and gesturing toward the cliff. On the rocky point, Colum stood abruptly, gawking at the water where the truck had been swallowed, clutching his penis.

The mother stared at Colum as if compelling him to be steady. His knees bent, he braced himself, but when his foot slipped, everything he reached for was slick. His eyes pursed shut when his cheekbone smacked the kelp, and his little body slid into the sea.

The mother's breasts surged a rush of milk. She dived, cold scalding her skull, and she could see nothing through a rush of water and a curtain of weeds that touched every part of her, and when she rose to the surface for air, there were others diving all around. Like gulls hunting.

In her family room, the mother peels North America from the plastic sheet of the world map.

There is value in visiting your torment, and there are numerous strategies for managing intrusive thoughts. Journalling for example.

Wegener's journal is buried beneath three hundred feet of ice in Greenland, where he died of heart failure due to overexertion during a polar mission. Scientists have since measured the magnetism of the ocean floor to show how it spreads. North America and Eurasia are drifting from each other at a rate of two-and-a-half centimetres per year.

I am getting nothing useful done today, the mother writes. *I lashed out at Colum. I am not fit to parent. My therapist recommends that I join a choir and rub a smooth stone.*

The mother positions North America on the wall and slides a ruler over the surface to remove air bubbles. It affixes smoothly except for one large bubble across Denver, Colorado. With a blade, she makes a careful slit and smooths the plastic to the wall, leaving a solid longitudinal wrinkle.

I am taking a long walk in the fresh air, she texts the husband. *Don't text while driving. Tell Colum I love him and that I am sorry.*

She peels South America next, but as she positions it, the triangular continent slinks and attaches to itself. As she pulls it apart, the map tears from the coast of Peru to the centre of Brazil. She should stop, the mother thinks. Reset. She should perform muscle relaxation exercises. The mother taught Colum a sequence of muscle relaxation exercises. "Love, when you feel anxious, when you feel anger, try tensing your core muscles, then release," she said.

The mother peels Europe from the plastic. Its boomerang shape tears through Poland and Romania, and she slaps the torn plastic onto the wall, palming the air bubbles into thick, hard, overlapping folds. She changes her mind and pulls the continent off the wall, ripping a patch of paint that exposes the chalky drywall beneath. The mother repositions Europe. Air bubbles form archipelagos throughout the continent and she shreds them with increasing haste, the blade cutting through the map to the wall. Russia is next. Astonishingly, the entire country detaches from the plastic without tearing, but as the mother presses it onto the wall, it buckles and sticks to its underside. The mother presses the plastic onto itself, distorting boundaries. She peels Africa carelessly now, and it static-clings to her sleeve. Clouded with pills of lint and wormy strands of hair, Africa is fitted neatly into the eastern coastline of North America. Ignoring her tears, she rips the other islands and continents from the plastic, and presses them into empty spaces on the wall, skewed and sideways, overlapping oceans and landmasses, air bubbles blistering ubiquitously.

The mother can see the reflection of her pinched face in the puzzled island of the world. She lowers her shoulders, tilts her chin, is transfixed by the ugly beauty of the distorted map. She slackens then, collapses, curls, weeps in savage rhythms, and when finally, the wave passes, she presses her wet cheek to the wall and clings as if glued to the world she has made.

G-LOC

Once upon a time there were two military kids, Jules and Siobhan.

I'm Jules.

Siobhan had a bunk bed with a built-in shelf where she kept the rocks and glass we collected — mostly Labradorite and shards of a school bus window that we came across one time. Her dad was deployed to Kosovo, or maybe Bosnia, and I was sleeping over at her house when her mom woke us up and took us outside in our pyjamas. We were wrapped in blankets so that the only thing touching the cold was our eyes. That night, the sky swirled green and blue; lights hovering and morphing. Those lights and their silence are bigger than anything you can say.

. . . .

In the nineties, military kids under eighteen were issued special compasses for coping with remote postings. The compasses could be attached around our wrist, or ankle, or any body part so long as it registered a pulse. They gave us special skills, those compasses. Powers, really. During the first week of arriving at CFB Goose Bay, Mom, Dad, and I waited in line at the Military Family Resource Centre with other newly posted families to receive our compasses. The rules were that we could not swap our compasses with other military kids, and it was absolutely forbidden to allow the civilian kids to meddle with them. The compasses were to be returned at the end of the posting.

Siobhan's skill was Magnetism. Mine was Chameleon. Other military kids got Ultra Vision, Flexibility, Telekinesis. The idea was that these compasses would help us assimilate with the local civilian kids. The reality was that the civilian kids were curious about us for about a week, and that was it. A lot of those kids had been friends forever, and they knew we'd be moving away in two or three years.

With her new Magnetism skill, Siobhan could slide a tin mug across the table in the cafeteria, open and close blinds in the classrooms. Outside, she'd stick her hands in the dirt, and as the sand fell away, iron ore filings covered her fingers, which were always puffy and scabby because she chewed her nails. "I give you ferrous sand," she said. "Iron ore from the very earth we walk upon." She said it like a magician.

My Chameleon skill made me blend with my surroundings. The shades of my clothing, my hair, my skin, shifted so slowly that people didn't usually see it happening. I could see it, the gradual darkening or lightening. I quickly noticed that one of two things happened when I switched on my compass and blended. Either the other kids seemed to forget that I was there, or they became familiar with me, like they'd known me forever. Vicki Coady was one of the popular girls in my class. She didn't even look at me until one day I turned on my Chameleon, and she told me all about an old bus her dad had bought for parts. It was parked in her backyard. Most of the seats were removed and they fit a picnic table inside where they played Crazy Eights. She had parties in the bus. It was like a bus cabin.

Siobhan was my first best friend. To this day actually, Siobhan is the best friend I ever had. Her father, Mr. D, was a NATO pilot from Germany, and Siobhan was an only child like me. My dad was an air traffic controller from Moose Jaw, Saskatchewan, and from age ten to twelve (twelve and a half, actually), I lived in 3A, and Siobhan lived in 3B of a PMQ duplex on Birchall Street in Goose Bay. It took exactly seven minutes and twenty-eight seconds for us to ride our bikes to the chain-link, barbed-wire fence that enclosed the runway. Every so often, I'm twelve again, and Siobhan and I are gripping the runway fence waiting for takeoff. Her dad waves from the cockpit as his Phantom II is taxied to the platform. Seven or eight jets take off in a row, tearing across the runway, and it's one explosion after the other. We stand shoulder to shoulder, fingers poked inside the diamonds as the thunder sweeps over the whole place and fills our stomachs. Airburst, boom in our chests, sand grit between our teeth, and the barbed wire rattles above our heads. Even the ground vibrates, and fumes from the planes turn air to water. Our eyes close. We are in a rocket's blast vibration. After the final jet, it all fades to nothing. Contrails streak grey-white before they feather, and it's so quiet we hear flags clanking on their poles. Siobhan says something like, "The force of those aircraft is nothing short of phenomenal." She took such pride in her English vocabulary, used words like extraordinary and sacrosanct. Sometimes, she started a sentence with, 'I suspect.'

My mother was a high-school music teacher, but there were no jobs at local schools, and the extreme cold gave her back pain. She panicked when jets flew at sonic speed, those explosions when they broke the sound barrier. Sometimes she was so scared she vomited. There is a dank, stale-bread smell that always reminds me of her housecoat and our house on Birchall Street. Mom thought a jet would crash on our house. Once, we were watching TV and she started to cry. My skin and my clothes turned greenish grey so quickly that I felt nauseous. All of a sudden, we were sitting on the floor of a green-lit room that was flooded. Our legs were underwater, and a receiver of a black telephone with a winding cord floated next to me. Mom stared straight ahead, and I felt so heavy that I couldn't move. My sweater tightened around my chest. When Mom looked at me, her eyes were like pebbles. That was the first time I realized that my Chameleon skill could latch onto moods and create wild imaginings. To anyone who noticed, I just blended with my surroundings, but I had these visions. I never used my Chameleon around Mom after that day watching TV.

Siobhan had a trampoline in her backyard, which was connected to my backyard. It had been left by the last military family, because its measurements exceeded the maximum allowable by the moving trucks, according to Siobhan. Once, during a winter storm, the trampoline blew hellbent across the base, ended up outside the terminal. Ms. D followed it with her camera as it rolled over snowbanks, powdered snow in its wake. It wagon-wheeled past the AVRO Vulcan aircraft that was mounted on a concrete plinth. *Click.* Her picture made it onto the front page of *The Labradorian*, and she framed it and added it to the collage of Labrador photographs she had on display above the stairs in their house.

Siobhan and I lay on her trampoline one time in late summer or fall, staring at the cloudless sky. I switched on my Chameleon, and it was like we were floating in clouds.

"Your skin has a blue tint. I can see it." Siobhan propped on her elbow to examine me. She bit into the skin of her ring finger.

"It's like we're floating."

Siobhan rooted in her pocket for her model F-18 jet.

"Why blue? Why not the colour of the trampoline?"

"I don't know. Sky's so big I guess."

She tried to get me to control my Chameleon, but I couldn't, nor could I control where my imagination went. All I could do was switch on my compass and wait to see what happened. The longer I left it on, the more I could sense people's moods, and the more the visions evolved. If I left it on for too long, I became tired, like my brain was wool. I also became tired of being invisible, because that's what it felt like, blending. Mostly, I turned on my Chameleon when it was just Siobhan and me, or when I was at her house, which was most days. She always wanted details.

"We're floating? Like flying?"

"Feels like it."

"See, Jules, it's engine thrust versus gravity," she said. "They take off. They accelerate. Straight up. Combat departure." Her tiny F-18 levitated above her palm, then shot past my face, straight up. "Those jets push against the very *brink* of stability," she said, looking up. "The very *brink,* and you positively *cannot* believe the G-force on the pilots." After a few seconds, the jet zipped back and landed in her hand. "The force of gravity can make the pilots lose consciousness. G-LOC! Gravity-induced loss of consciousness." Her eyes were wide and dramatic. "G-LOC!"

Siobhan had control over her Magnetism. She would think up new tricks to show the civilian kids so that we'd get invited to the bus cabin. When she concentrated, the muscles around her eyelids tightened, and she'd gaze off into a corner. She'd suck a piece of her curly brown hair so that the corner of her mouth was always mottled and chapped. Her hair was usually a tangled mess. She didn't care. She didn't care about any of those things, or clothes and stuff, which I liked because I didn't care about those things either.

....

One time, in the woods behind the PMQs, Siobhan was ahead of me on her bike, the back of her neck sunburned and bitten up from the mosquitoes. We came across a clearing with a half-built jet-fuel tank. It was a giant cylinder, open at the top, and we climbed all the way up the winding steps. Scaffolding was set up inside like a skeleton. I remember looking up from the inside of the tank at a perfect pie of blue sky. We ran around, our steps echoing. Siobhan pressed her ear to the tank and knocked with her fist. "Anybody home?" she said. Toolboxes and equipment, a yellow plastic stereo, and sections of metal pipe were set off to one side beneath a tarp, and she poked around, pulling things out. It didn't matter that I told her not to. She picked up a blow torch, unstrapped the hose, looked straight into it. With her Magnetism, she drew a section of pipe into her hand and another on top, and another, until she was balancing eight or nine pieces of pipe. She dropped them and the whole tank ba-rrringed and hummed and kept ba-rrringing and humming. We raced up the scaffolding, Siobhan yanking the back of my jeans to get me over the high sections. Running down the outer steps, I slipped, and my back scraped on the perforated metal as I slid into Siobhan. She grabbed the railing, attaching to it with her Magnetism, and stopped us both from falling all the way down. My back and head burned as we rode our bikes home.

"Jesus Christ!" Siobhan said as I lifted my shirt in the upstairs bathroom. Mom was downstairs watching *The Price Is Right*. "Jesus Christ!" she said again, sounding like someone older. I had a bruise and peeled skin from my belt to my neck. Siobhan washed my back with wads of wet tissue that crumbled and fell to the floor. Water dribbled down the back of my jeans. "There we go," she said, rubbing cream that made my eyes burn, taping cloth bandages over my back. "That should be sufficient."

"I'm a mummy in Egypt." .

"Just don't tell your mother. She'll have a heart attack. She is quite the worrywart."

"She's not."

"I heard my mother say she is a worrywart," Siobhan said as she helped me with my shirt. "Why doesn't your father help her? He helps my mother all the time. The Christmas lights, the car, the broken step in our basement. He doesn't need to. My mother is quite capable, actually. One time in Germany, she climbed up a ladder with a giant nutcracker for the roof and th . . ."

I was not in the mood for Germany stories, and what right did Siobhan have to say that my mom was a worrywart? For Mom, Labrador was dangerous predators, toxic fumes, heavy metals. Wolves in the woods, bears at the dump, old military barracks collapsing, nuclear storage bunkers, snowmobiles sinking through ice. After the jets, the worst of her horrors were the rotator-blade snowploughs. A few years ago, one had minced three kids while they were inside their snow fort. Plus, Mom had no friends in Goose Bay. Not one friend that I can remember.

"I'm having a vision, Siobhan," I said, interrupting her.

Her eyes widened. "Tell me."

"It's you."

"What is it?"

"Your entire body is wrapped in cloth like a mummy, and your hands are little balls, like you have no fingers."

"Like my fingers are chopped off?" She made fists and held them in front of her face.

"Like you chewed them to the knuckles."

"Gnarly." She lowered her hands to her side, gazed at the floor. "I want you to tell your father to stop helping my mom."

"Okay. I'll tell him," I said. I was impatient, thinking Siobhan was being childish.

. . . .

Siobhan's mom, Ms. D, painted their living-room ceiling rust orange and the walls mud green. I'd never been inside a PMQ that wasn't white. She had plants on the floor, on stands, and hanging from the ceiling, and the furniture was wicker, with cushions that had upside-down elephants on them. There was a cuckoo clock with boys and girls on teeter-totters that sounded like a fairy-tale every hour. The front room often filled with ten or twelve women, other pilots' wives. They ate cheese, olives, and crackers, and drank pots of tea or bottles of wine depending on the time of day. Ms. D always invited my mom, but she didn't ever go. I don't know why, exactly. It's not like she had other things to do. She was usually on the other side of the wall watching *Murder She Wrote* or *The Price Is Right* in her stale-smelling housecoat.

Siobhan had three guinea pigs who lived in a cage on a table in the kitchen. She nuzzled them with her nose, and even kissed them on the lips. "They are exceptionally intelligent," she said. Her favourite was the female guinea pig she'd named Comfy, who made sounds to signal hunger or happiness. To signal fear, she'd grind her teeth, shake from her core. Siobhan also had a one-year-old black Lab dog named Oscar, and one summer, Oscar pulled the guinea-pig cage off the table.

We were on the trampoline when we heard the crash. Barks, squeaks, panicked scrabble of nails on parquet. Oscar yelped in chase, sliding around corners, smashing into walls and chairs and plant stands. Broken ceramic and plants and dirt on the floor. Siobhan screamed at Oscar, who only got more excited. Ms. D ran up from the basement with a frozen ham in her arms, dropped it to the counter. With one hand, she scooped a guinea pig from behind the table, with the other, she picked up the cage. Siobhan caught the second guinea pig and used her Magnetism to knock a folding chair to block Comfy, but Oscar was on the creature, and she scurried for the open basement door. The stairs were deadly steep. Siobhan raced down, three steps at a time, to find Comfy in a curled heap on the cement floor, shaking, panting shallow squeaks. She died that evening, and we buried her in the backyard. Ms. D took a picture as Siobhan magnetized handfuls of ferrous sand and placed them around the grave in circular mounds. The picture hung on the wall next to the trampoline in the storm and the two of us bundled in blankets under the northern lights.

Ms. D was beautiful, with sharp cheekbones, short brunette hair, and a long neck. She'd steer me by the elbow and sit me down for a bowl of soup or stew. "You. Are. My . . . precious person," she said to Siobhan, touching both her cheeks and smelling her head. Ms. D had a gentle kind of roughness. She rubbed my back when she hugged me, or pet my hand like a paw; her own hands dry and chapped. In summer, she wore sleeveless shirts. There were three moles on her left arm that made me think of an animal, like a leopard or a lynx. Around her ankle, she wore a thin black leather band, which she kept on all the time, even when she took us swimming at the

Rec Centre pool on Fridays. There was a diving board at the pool that I never built up the courage to try. Siobhan jumped off it many times, headfirst. She tried to get me to try it. "Jules, it is truly a thrill to behold," she said.

. . . .

It was important to Siobhan that we made friends with the local civilian kids. At school, she pronounced words differently, and she smiled with a closed-mouth grin that was fake and sad. Her voice changed too. When she spoke to the civilian kids, she was extra cheery, like anything was possible, and it made her sound naive. A lot of the kids had snowmobiles, and after school, they'd meet at Johnny Hill to ride in the trails. They'd talk about their plans in front of us, never inviting us to join. One time, in the cafeteria, some kids were sitting near us, making plans. Siobhan was gnawing into a hangnail, and she switched on her compass and made a trash can levitate. When the others noticed, they started whispering and laughing. They'd seen her do this before. At first, they'd ask her to do other things, and Siobhan might snake a chain of paper clips across the floor or roll a book trolly in the library, but on that day, they made fun of her. Siobhan's face flushed as she lowered the can and sat back with a sad grin. I moved my tray to her side of the table and turned on my compass, shocking her a little because I rarely activated my Chameleon at school.

"Anything?" She sat up in her seat.

"Patience."

My colours faded to a pale beige, and then it happened. One of my most memorable Chameleon visions. "It's a tree trunk — like a massive one, in the middle of the table."

"Really? It's growing?"

"No. No leaves. It's dead, I think." Then I noticed the ants. "Ants. Big, big ants."

"Extraordinary! They must be wood ants. See if you can see their trails. They eat trails."

"Yes, the wood has lines all over. It's kind of pretty."

"Extraordinary!" she said a second time.

Vicki Coady and two of her friends sat next to us. "What's going on?"

I switched off my compass and the tree faded. "Nothing."

"Jules's compass makes her have these extraordinary visions. There was just a giant tree trunk right here on the table, covered in wood ants."

"Whoa, like, can you control them?"

"No not really."

"Like, what kinds of visions?"

"Different things." I was exhausted.

"So, I'm having a party next weekend in my bus. You should come."

I shrugged, not interested, but Siobhan said we'd come, and it was settled.

....

On the night of the party, Dad dropped us off at Vicki's house, which was in the town near the base. The streets were snow-packed, and the air was so cold that when I inhaled, I could feel the frost in my nose and throat. The bus was in the back-yard with a generator running. Most of the kids were already in the bus, sitting at the picnic table, eating chips. A boombox was on the floor in the corner playing Samantha Fox's "Touch Me." The windows of the bus were covered in frost.

"Okay, that's everyone. Time for Spin-the-Bottle," Vicki said, as she took our hats and mitts.

We sat on the floor in a circle. Vicki was the first to spin, and it landed on a guy named Todd Broomfield. In the middle of the circle, Vicki and Todd kissed. Her tongue flicked out of her mouth and the others cheered. When guys spun and landed on other guys, they had to spin again. Girls gave girls pecks on cheeks. There was extra hollering and hooting during kissing when hands slipped up shirts or touched bums. It was all stupid. I wanted to leave.

A guy named Dean spun the bottle and it landed on Siobhan.

"I'm not kissing that," he said.

There was laughter and Siobhan grinned, rose onto her knees, and grabbed the bottle.

"You are a dickhead," Siobhan said, using a word I'd never heard her use before. She spun the bottle, and it landed on

Jimmy Mac. Jimmy was quiet and shy, and his parents owned the only Chinese restaurant in town. Vicki stood up in the middle of the circle.

"Okay, the game is now moving to the next level. Instead of kissing, it's hickeys."

I didn't have my compass switched on, but I became alert to a collective consciousness around me, as though the others knew something that I didn't.

Siobhan and Jimmy stood in the middle of the circle. She was taller than him, so she bent over, placed her hands on his shoulders and started sucking on his neck, her eyes wide open. Everyone yelled, and Siobhan kept going until Jimmy pushed her away.

"Ow!" He rubbed his neck where Siobhan had left a brownish, purple mark.

"I'm not playing this anymore." Jimmy backed out of the circle.

Vicki's father stuck his head into the bus. "Fire's ready, Vic!"

"S'mores!" Everyone followed Vicki to the backyard where benches and chairs had been placed around the fire. Snow was falling.

"Make something float, Siobhan," Vicki said.

"Like what?"

"I don't know. The soccer ball."

"It's gotta be something metal."

"The pitchfork!" someone yelled.

"I don't want to poke someone's eye out."

"The rake." Vicki pointed to a plastic rake with a metal handle leaning on the side of a shed. Siobhan switched her compass on and floated the rake, making it flip and spin. She floated it above our heads, holding it above Dean for a little longer. Then she hovered it over the fire making it tick tock.

"It's melting! The plastic!"

Strings of green plastic dripped in globs on peoples' jeans and boots as Siobhan tried to float the rake away from the fire. A chunk of burning plastic landed on Jimmy's forehead and he wailed in pain. Jumping off the bench, he staggered around trying to wipe the burning plastic off his face, but it stuck to his hand like glue. His screams were like that of a baby animal. Vicki's parents came running.

"What on earth? Jesus, Mary, and Joseph!" Vicki's mother shrieked when she saw Jimmy's face. She crouched over him holding his arms down, rubbing a handful of snow on his face. "George, call his parents." Jimmy squirmed violently, pawing at his face, screaming for her to let him go. He looked up at the sky and closed his eyes, pushing away from her. The skin on his face was mottled and pink, folding over itself in thin ripples.

When she found out what happened, Vicki's mother yelled at Siobhan in front of everyone. She yelled at her about the hickey too. When Dad arrived to take us home, Vicki's mother was still red in the face. Siobhan was staring off into the sky, wide-eyed.

"She burnt his face. His poor face. And his hands. That military compass nonsense should not be allowed. I'm telling you right now, it won't be allowed here again, Jesus, Mary, and Joseph."

Siobhan winced when Dad put his hand on her shoulder. "I'm sure it was an accident," he said.

"The neck was no accident then." Vicki's mother glared at Siobhan. "You should have seen the poor fellow's neck. That was no accident. It's all-out violence is what it is, and that Jimmy is the shyest little creature. Look at her, she's not even sorry."

Siobhan was silent. She rooted her hands in her pockets.

"I'll let her mother know what happened. Her father is overseas for another two months."

Vicki's mother's eyes shot to Siobhan. "She's an odd one, that child."

On our drive home, the car smelled bitter like a damp towel because Dad had rushed out of hockey practice to pick us up.

"Maybe you might want to turn the compasses off for a while until we get this settled. We might have to file a report."

Siobhan stared out the window. "You know, I saw you one time, when you took us to the drugstore. I saw you looking at a naked woman in a magazine. I saw you do that."

Dad looked at Siobhan in his rear-view mirror. He started to say something, but she interrupted him.

"And for your information, my mother does not require your help, and she will decide when I can or cannot use my Magnetism, and you do not need to involve yourself."

I switched my compass on in the back seat and as I faded, fuzzy green mildew crept over the windows and ceiling of the car. I felt warm and sweaty. I wanted to tell Siobhan about it, but it was hard to breathe, and she didn't want to talk. She stared out the window scrunching her face. When we got home, Siobhan ran to her house, and Dad followed her. Mom and I ate supper together — microwave pizzas with green peas, and then we bundled up and went outside to look at the northern lights. They spread over the entire sky, hanging like fluorescent fog. I told her about Spin-the-Bottle and the rake and the way Vicki's mom yelled at Siobhan.

"The lights are beautiful tonight," she said. "Hard to believe how they morph." Mom gazed up at the blue and green lights, their shapes shifting slowly. "They morph," she said. "It's like people. People morph. Think how much a person morphs in their lifetime."

"She was mean to Siobhan, Mom. The way she yelled at her, right in her face yelling. In front of everyone."

"Sweetie, all Vicki's mom can see is how good Siobhan has it."

....

The following week in school, someone drew a picture on the bathroom stall of two girls with their pants down. "Siobhan fingering Jules." Both stick figures had big round heads and sharp triangles for teeth. One had scribbles of curly hair. Lightning bolts shot out in all directions. In capital letters: PSYCHO LESBOS.

After school that day, Siobhan and I were on the snowbank at the end of our street. We'd made a winding, sliding trail with our butts when the snowplough first piled up the bank, and around the back, we carved out a fort that was sheltered from wind. It was so quiet, I could hear my own heart, and the high-pitched beeps of the airport. Snowmobiles buzzed in the trails. "Idiots," Siobhan said as she dug the heel of her boot into the snow. Her cheeks were glossy pink.

"They'll forget about everything in a few weeks," I said.

"Quite frankly, I could care less about all of them. They don't know anything. They've never been out of this place, and it's likely they'll never leave. I've lived in three countries already, and soon I'll be moving out of this dump."

"You're posted?" I thought Siobhan had another two years like me.

"No, but I mean, you know, we'll move eventually."

Siobhan continued to dig a hole with the heel of her boot. "I am going to be a pilot. A fighter pilot like my father."

"Are there girl fighter pilots?"

"I could be the first."

"I would die. I would not want to fly one of those jets."

"Oh, but it's a truly thrilling sensation, Jules. They train their bodies. When Dad gets back, we can go in the centrifuge machine. You'll love it, Jules. Can you imagine us flying together?"

We did imagine flying together. We built a Lego diorama of CFB Goose Bay on Siobhan's basement floor and then we played Cold War. We built the exact number of living quarters, pale blue and green two-story duplexes. We dribbled real grass and sand for the shared lawns and sand driveways. We cut up moving boxes and painted little strips of cardboard for the roads and the runways, the parade square. When Mr. D got back, he helped us build the Strategic Air Command Weapons Storage Area, which Siobhan would say in an evil, Dracula voice, "Nuke Storage Area." It was surrounded by fences (more paper clips), topped with barbed wire (steel wool), and inside the fences, a guard house, three warehouses, six guard towers, and five sand-covered bunkers for the Fat Man atomic bombs. We used marbles for the plutonium pits. Siobhan would say, "Demon core," also in her evil voice. Mr. D told us about the B-50 bomber that was carrying nuclear bombs from Goose Bay to Arizona in the 1950s when its four engines malfunctioned and it dropped its payload into the St. Lawrence River, contaminating it with uranium.

"Mayday! Mayday!" Siobhan yelled, flying a bomber across the St. Lawrence River (Star Wars pillowcase). "Declaring an emergency. Left two engines have failed. Dropping payload!"

She dropped a marble into the river. With her Magnetism she flew planes around her basement. I played along with my visions of flying the planes at sonic speed and flying them in the nape of the earth. Ms. D brought shortbread cookies or grapes or muffins, her camera around her neck; she took pictures of us at war. We pretended she was a Russian spy.

....

On the first Saturday of December, the windows of my house were covered in a veil of frost, so when Dad backed the car out of the driveway the headlights swept over us, illuminating each tiny crystal of ice. Mom curled on the couch, bundled in blankets. Standing by the window, I melted a circle of frost with my palm, the cold numbing my skin. The screen door banged, and Siobhan appeared in our living room.

"Jules! Cold War?"

I looked at my mother, her face waxy, pimples around her chin and on her forehead.

"I'm gonna stay home and watch *Annie*. Dad's on nightshift."

"Yeah, my father's flying tonight. Testing the new NVGs."

Earlier that day, Mr. D had taken us to the hangars. We climbed on the jets, sat in the cockpit. He showed us the new night-vision goggles. Then he brought us to the training centre to see the centrifuge machine, a small cockpit-sized capsule attached to a mechanical arm that rotated, spinning the capsule at increasing speeds to simulate forces of gravity.

"So, who's first?"

"Jules!" Siobhan was giddy. I wasn't sure about it.

Siobhan's dad picked out a G-suit. The G-suit was tight around my legs, and he tightened it around my waist so that I could hardly breathe. "Can't let blood pool in your legs and abdomen. Gotta keep the blood in the brain." He pointed to his head as he said this, and then slapped my helmet visor shut. Orange world. Mr. D helped me into the capsule. "It's going to get heavy," he said. "Breathe forcefully, flex your muscles, your calves, your shoulders, your thighs. Keep the blood in the brain."

The capsule closed around me.

As it started to spin, I sank into the seat. Siobhan and her dad blended to lines like horizontal lasers that encircled me. My heart pounded heavy, and my body deflated into the seat. The last of my peripheral vision was the flap of skin on my cheeks as my face dragged, contorted under the pressure. I didn't feel human. Shadows deepened around me, and my vision narrowed until it was gone. Faithful departure.

In the centrifuge machine, blood was forced away from my brain, breaking a spell. What was clear was that I could not hold onto anything. Not love, not friendship, not even family; that each of these things would morph and fade like a mood, like fluorescent lights in the black sky. Isolation was the only thing that was solid and complete. It was the only thing I could trust.

"Jules, wake up! Jules! You G-LOC'd!" Siobhan smiled down at me, shaking my shoulders. She wrapped her arms around my neck and squeezed.

Somehow, inside that moment, as I slipped beneath consciousness, I knew that I was connected to a peril that was to come. Even though it was hours before the Phantom II plane would go down on the night that my dad was controlling the terminal and Siobhan's dad was flying.

Before the crash bell would sound and the Operations Officer would telephone Ms. D and say, "Gather everyone," and by everyone, he would mean the wives. I would sense the dread before Ms. D barged through our front door to find Mom, Siobhan, and me watching *Annie* on the couch. "A plane is down," she'd say, as gusts of snow and frosty air whipped around the black leather band on her ankle. Before the wives would sit in the rust-orange room with the mud-green ceiling, in wicker chairs, on the floor, and Mom, on the bottom step, watching the others through the railing of the banister as if she was safe, because her husband did not fly jets. The curtains of the front window would flare and fall each time the door burst open.

I sensed the changes that would come. Before Siobhan would yell, "Which plane? Which pilot?" and Ms. D would tell her to wait, and Siobhan would glare at the boiling kettle on the stove, float it at eye level, and fly it across the room into the wall making a Fat Man detonation of boiling water and steam. Before she'd run through the cluster of anxious wives, pass my mother on the stairs, knock three hanging picture frames so that they tumbled downstairs, ricocheting shards of glass. Before a polygon of broken glass would slide down the back of Mom's housecoat, pierce the cotton of her nightgown and the skin below her shoulder blade, making droplets of blood that would leave a stain. When Mom would hardly react to the blood, but Siobhan would half-scream, half-cry, "If you weren't always in your disgusting housecoat, your husband would love you instead of my mother."

I sensed, inside that moment, the end of our friendship. I sensed my lifelong connection to aloneness. In Siobhan's house, the wives would show support and hope for each other, but in truth, the hope would be for themselves; the only thing they shared was desperation.

When the Operations Officer arrived with Padre Larry, announcing that it was Buster whose plane went down, that they'd located the aircraft but had no comms, that the ground rescue crew would be at the crash site in approximately ninety minutes. When Buster's wife, Emma, walked to the front window, drew the curtain, stared at the frost and said, "It's twenty-eight degrees below zero."

In the end, Buster ejected, survived the crash and the cold with two broken ribs and frostbite on his left eyelid. He did not crash because of a gravity-induced loss of consciousness; he crashed because his night-vision goggles malfunctioned.

Later that week, there was a party at the Officers' Mess to celebrate the engineers who had designed the new ejection seat. The plane had crashed in a field less than a kilometre outside of the town, plowing a crater in the earth the length of six school buses.

Mom had a complete breakdown. For weeks after the crash, she cried uncontrollably. We didn't ever talk about what Siobhan had said. When the jets flew above the house, Mom howled, covered her ears, curled into a ball. She told my dad she couldn't do it; she couldn't live there anymore. We got a compassionate posting to Ottawa and were scheduled to move out of Goose Bay in early February.

Siobhan and I didn't talk about the move. I think we pretended it wasn't going to happen. One night over Christmas holidays, we fell asleep watching *E.T.* I woke up because she was leaning on my arm, and it was cramped. "Stay with me," she said, without opening her eyes. I didn't move my arm until my hand went completely numb.

On moving day, Siobhan and I were sitting on our front step. The movers lifted boxes and furniture and my bike into the back of the moving truck that would take our life to Ottawa. I'd never moved in the winter before. I returned my compass when we signed out of the base and Siobhan turned in her compass as well.

"I'm done with Magnetism. Are you going to miss your compass?"

"Not really. I only used it with you anyway. Anywhere else, I got so tired."

"The best thing, in your new school, is to just tell jokes," she said, which irritated me, because I didn't tell jokes. I didn't even know any jokes.

"That's dumb."

"I mean it, tell jokes, and people will like you automatically. Learn some jokes." Siobhan gave me a small square box of chocolates. "It's been great knowing you these past few years."

"Thanks. Good luck being the first girl pilot."

"Just wait! You'll see."

. . . .

It was early spring when Ms. D called us in Ottawa. Siobhan had climbed to the top of a jet-fuel tank and meddled with the valves until one shot open, smashing her in the face. The orbital rim of her left eye had been crushed and she'd lost the use of that eye. She'd suffered minor brain damage from the fumes and was in the hospital under observation. I spoke with her for a few minutes. Her voice was nasally. She told me the kids at school were friendly to her now, and that Jimmy Mac had knit her a scarf.

I pictured Siobhan riding her bike through the trails by herself with a patch on her eye.

That summer, her family moved back to Germany. We wrote letters for a year or two, but her letters didn't sound like her. She wrote about orange-flavoured chocolate and the chickens they kept in their backyard. Mom said her brain was probably changed forever.

Usually, when I think of Siobhan, I feel sad. She didn't die, but it was like she did. I never saw her again. Every few years, we left one life in one place and started another life from scratch, in another place. I have no idea where she is now, if she married, had kids. I can't imagine that she ever became a pilot. Pilots need two top-notch eyes.

What I can imagine is her running on that diving board, leaping straight up, rising higher and higher until she spreads into a cartwheel yelling "Mayday! Mayday!" Us racing our bikes through the sandy trails, our fingers clenching the chain-link fence. Siobhan raises her arms like a maestro and makes the jets blast off, shoots them straight up against gravity into a silent blue sky, joins them together in formation to manoeuvre a swift combat departure, before they vanish to nothing.

IN THE SKIN OF A LAMB

Husband is deployed to Kuwait for six months, and immediately upon his departure I order a new vibrator called The Womanizer. The name makes me grind my teeth. I might have taken this response as a prophesy of irritation; a foreshadowing of titillation so complex and marvellous I would struggle to articulate my own sense of something off-kilter, something unsatisfactory. But alas, The Womanizer arrives on my doorstep on the same day that Husband settles into his base camp and encounters his first camel spider, which, remarkably, bears resemblance in shape, colour, and size (approximately six inches in length) to my shiny new vibrator.

The first element of dissatisfaction I encounter with my new vibrator is the inequality that exists between the phallic piece and the circular, suction-cup, clitoral-stimulation piece. The phallic piece has twelve modes. Twelve different rhythms of vibration from the wave to the cha-cha to the old faithful jackhammer. The clitoral stimulator has one mode. One mode of air and suction to service more than eight thousand nerve endings that live inside the tender folds of the clitoris. It gives me pause. I contemplate the state of the world around me. This elliptical world in which the G-spot is king and the clitoris, the indisputable hub, central intelligence, and headquarters of female pleasure is a secondary character. G-spot, schmee spot.

I calculate the time zone difference between Eastern Standard Time and Arabia Standard Time in order to discuss this gross injustice with Husband. Husband says, stiffly, that he is not in a position to have such a lewd conversation.

Lewd? I say. Please. So, what shall we talk about? The ancient Greeks? Camel spiders? Mahsa Amini?

How is your father? Husband says.

Father is good, I say.

Father is great. He saved an orphan lamb last week. One sheep birthed a stillborn lamb on the same day that another sheep died giving birth to a lamb that survived. Father removed the skin of the dead lamb and secured it to the orphaned lamb. "'Twas like putting a sweater on the little thing," he said triumphantly. The mother sheep gradually took to the orphan lamb, which was wearing her scent. She nourished the lamb with her milk, and as such, the story concluded with an abundant flourish of the infinite joys of nature.

I asked Father to consider whether the poor mother sheep might have been exhausted after such a traumatic birthing experience. Given the choice, I said, perhaps she would have preferred some rest and self-care instead of being duped into raising an orphan. Father asked me why in the name of God I always had to be so militant. He had to go then. He had towels on the line, and it looked like rain. A master changer of subjects, a shape-shifter within the confines of conversation, Father had towels on the line, and so he hung up.

Well, you are militant, Husband says.

Am not.

Are too.

....

Years ago, I was fascinated by an article in *The Guardian* that revealed new information concerning the death of famous militant suffragette Emily Wilding Davison. Davison died from her injuries after being trampled by King George V's horse during the 1913 Derby, and over the course of time, history had its way with her. She was a suicidal radical. She was a reckless anarchist. She was a brave martyr. She was confused and didn't notice the barrage of horses barrelling toward her as she traversed the track. Please. In 2013, a new study of three separate newsreels revealed that Davison wasn't attempting to pull down the king's horse when she bolted onto the racetrack. She was trying to attach the suffragette flag to the royal racehorse's bridle.

The horse fell but rose and completed the course without a jockey. The jockey suffered a mild concussion and claimed that for the rest of his life he was haunted by the face of Emily Davison.

. . . .

Did you know, Husband says, that the camel spider can run up to sixteen kilometers an hour?!

That's horrific, I say.

They are not true spiders, Husband says. They do not create silk. They are members of the class Arachnida but are actually Solifuges. They hide in shadows; they eat small birds. How is Daughter?

Daughter is troubled, I say. She fell off a horse. Twice. She injured her hip. She is suffering. The horses at the stable are out of sorts because of the lockdowns, and the isolation is getting to them. Daughter says they are not like themselves. They are nervous and on edge and easily spooked. Twice, Daughter was thrown by a horse she loved and trusted. She is injured and heartbroken and no longer wishes to ride.

What did Coach recommend? Husband says.

Coach recommended she get back in the saddle. I insisted that she is the master of her own timeline. Daughter said my dramatic tendency was not helping the situation.

You are dramatic, Husband says.

I would like her to be the leading actor in her own life, I say.

Dramatic, Husband says.

You are dramatic, I say.

Not even, Husband says.

I am struggling with the isolation and loneliness of single parenting in these fraught and troublesome times, I say. Mahsa Amini was twenty-two. Did you know that? Did you know they said she was acting? They used batons. She was twenty-two, Husband. She was visiting her brother.

I am sorry, Husband says. You are not dramatic. Have you had any time to yourself? What are you reading?

Deborah Levy.

Too cerebral, not comforting, Husband says. Why not send the kids to Grandparents and watch a movie?

You are wrong, I say. Levy nourishes my soul with her graceful and lyrical rumination on such questions as, What is a woman for? What should a woman be? But I see what you mean, Husband. Which movie do you recommend?

Troy.

Too masculine and violent.

It's Brad Pitt, Husband says. It's ancient Greece.

Okay, I'll watch it with my new vibrator.

You do you, Husband says.

....

The movie *Troy* is best enjoyed while conducting secondary activities such as unloading the dishwasher, peeling carrots and potatoes, and switching the laundry from the washing machine to the dryer, hanging to dry the delicate items of course — we were not raised by wolves — all of which can be achieved during the numerous archaic battle scenes between the Trojans and the Spartans. I significantly enhance the lovemaking scene between Achilles (Brad Pitt) and his abducted priestess war-prize lover with the aid of The Womanizer vibrator. Although underwhelming in its variety of clitoral stimulation modes, The Womanizer is equipped with technology to live long and prosper for two and a half hours, which almost covers the duration of Wolfgang Petersen's epic Hollywood interpretation of Homer's *Iliad*.

I find myself wondering, who is Helen of Troy? A legendary beauty — the face that launched a thousand ships. A victim of abduction or a shameful adulteress? How did she live? How did she die? What did she confide to her close friends? What were her deepest desires? Did she have close friends? Was she aware of the false gift horse? She is mostly presented as a secondary character through a prism of idealization that makes it impossible to unravel her truth.

....

With a bribe of a burger at her favourite downtown restaurant, I convince Daughter to accompany me for a day at the National Gallery. Despite her lack of enthusiasm for the museum, I am happy to spend the day together. There is a looming disconnect between us as of late. I am beginning to feel like a satellite orbiting her existence. Daughter is becoming less open, spending most of her free time in her room weaving friendship bracelets and watching *The Big Bang Theory*.

....

How are you doing? I ask Daughter. I mean, with your father being overseas.

Okay, Daughter says. She is annoyed, impatient, eye rolling. I don't really miss him, she says. I mean, I miss him, but it's not like I'm sad and depressed all the time. We text. We FaceTime. We are reading the *Divergent* series.

Daughter and Husband are one and the same.

You seem a bit off, I say, prying.

Mother.

I love you, I say.

Mother, please stop.

As such, the daughter vault of precious and unknowable material remains locked in the presence of an increasingly cumbersome mother gaze.

....

The National Gallery exhibit is called *Uninvited: Canadian Women Artists in the Modern Movement*. There is one piece by Paraskeva Clark that I am especially looking forward to. A large oil on canvas titled *Myself*.

My profound worship of Russian émigré Paraskeva Clark was born a few years ago when I learned of the Sampson-Matthews silkscreen project, which provided artwork for the armed services during the Second World War. Paraskeva contributed the landscape *Caledonian Farm in May*. An advocate for the importance of art during wartime, she featured celebrated female sniper Lieutenant Lyudmila Pavlichenko in a large canvas. She was appointed to depict the work of the Women's Division of the Royal Canadian Air Force and painted *Parachute Riggers* in 1947.

I imagine her as a young artist in Russia watching theatre performances in the factories, fairgrounds, and streets of pre-revolutionary Saint Petersburg, working in her father's shoe factory by day, attending art lessons by night, drawing plaster heads in charcoal and human figures in red chalk, creating vast neo-romantic theatre sets, painting her lips bright red. I tap into her grief and despondence while living with her in-laws in Paris following the tragic death of her husband. "In Paris, I worked very little by myself, just a few hours now and then stolen from housework," she wrote while single parenting her young son. "But my mind, my eyes were painting all the time." In her 1956 painting *Mother and Child*, a young woman sits at a table, holding a sleeping child. The woman rests her head in her left hand, a glass of tea within reach. Books and artists' tools litter the table, and an empty chair sits in the foreground. For whom or what is this vacant chair, I wonder, her dead husband or her infinite yearning?

Paraskeva Clark's painting *Myself* is a self-portrait of the artist when she was pregnant with her second child. It is mostly shades of grey and beige except for her signature bright red lips. I want to spend quality time with this larger-than-life depiction. I have important questions to ask her.

Outside the National Gallery, a giant, egg-carrying spider is cast in bronze. The sculpture, titled *Maman*, was inspired by the strength of the artist's mother with metaphors of spinning, weaving, nurturance, and protection. It stands thirty feet high, over thirty feet wide, and includes a sack of marble eggs.

....

Did you know, Husband says, it is a complete myth that camel spiders chase human beings?

I know nothing of these fake spiders, dear Husband, other than what you have so generously offered.

They chase shadows, Husband says. It's the shade they are after. Relief from the desert heat.

I can't imagine that such transient human shadows can provide much relief, I say.

You are right, Husband says. A fruitless chase, really. How was the museum?

Daughter thinks *Maman* is the stuff of nightmares, I say. She enjoyed climbing the creepy giant legs. Then she was hungry. Then she had cramps.

Did you visit the exhibit?

No. Sadly, no.

And the restaurant?

There was a video game near our table. A hunting game with a bulky orange plastic gun and a background scene with four deer in the forest. Incredulous deer eyes peering out from dense forest. Our server wore a camouflage patterned T-shirt that also had a deer, a massive buck with a prized set of antlers.

Server uniform? Husband says.

Daughter thought the same thing, I say. The waiter looked at the video game, shrugged sheepishly, and said it was a coincidence.

Before I forget, Husband says. Boy from school continues to hound Daughter.

Hound?

Lusting after her, Husband says. Won't leave her alone.

Why did she not bring this to me? I say, perplexed and hurt. I am here. You are in a desert on the other side of the world.

It's difficult to say. Altogether unknowable in fact. Please don't be upset, my love. It's the dynamic.

. . . .

For Easter, Daughter and I fly to Newfoundland to see Grand-father. On Sunday morning, depleted after the trip, and chronically weary of being a secondary human being within the realm of the Catholic church, I elect to skip mass. Daughter can go on my behalf, I say, supplicating. Grandfather's response has nothing to do with his deep disappointment in the face of my lapsed Catholicism. No no. Instead, he picks up the latest book by Lisa Moore, *This Is How We Love*. One of my favourites. Definitely on my top ten shelf. Top five even.

I still haven't read this one, Grandfather says.

But Father, I say, astounded. It's been out for more than a year.

This is how we throw punches.

While we fail to argue about my not attending Easter Sunday mass, Daughter prepares for the Passion of the Christ. She descends the stairs in skin-tight jeans that are so tight, I worry for the safety of her labia majora. The jeans are ripped below the kneecaps and across both thighs, and in this moment, I am rendered incapable. I simply cannot. I cannot conjure the words to explain to Grandfather that those kneecaps do not belong to me, nor do they belong to him. Furthermore, those thighs do not belong to the parishioners of Sacred Heart Parish. The kneecaps and thighs in question are the property of Daughter — full stop. But I am exhausted, and I tell Daughter she simply cannot wear the jeans. Not here, I say, not to mass on Easter Sunday, the day the good

Lord and Saviour rises from the dead to sit at the right hand of The Father. It would be a gesture of profound disrespect. Daughter asks if it is possible for me to be more of a hypocrite, and anyway she has nothing else to wear. Her only other pair of pants are the ones she wore in the stable yesterday, and they are covered in sheep manure. They reek.

Grandfather slowly bends to a kneeling position, opens the glass door of the wood stove, and manoeuvres a medium-sized log of birch onto the fire. I don't mind the smell of sheep, he says gently, and as he closes the door, the creak of its cast iron hinge resembles the wretched sound of a joyful swing set.

While they attend mass, I reread my favourite chapter of my favourite Deborah Levy book. The chapter is called "The Big Silver," and it features a forty-five-year-old man, a womanizer — the Big Silver, who fails in his attempt to seduce a young woman. The young woman is reading by herself at a restaurant when he interrupts her and invites her to join him for a night swim. She speaks in strange metaphors; he says she talks a lot. He is all oversight, the Big Silver, interrupting her train of thought. He changes the subject at his leisure. It does not occur to him, Levy writes, that the young woman came with a whole life and libido of her own. It does not occur to him that the young woman considers herself to be the lead character in this discourse between them. He may be the title of the chapter, but it is possible for the story to be about her. He does not consider that the strange metaphors she presents might represent an undisclosed hurt, because he is deaf and blind to her most intimate and important rhythms and modes. She will go down in his history as an attractive young woman who talked a lot. As for me, I am satisfied with the knowledge that she was able to shut him down and turn him off.

ROE V. CAVIAR

My thirteen-year-old daughter makes rules and tapes them to her bedroom door:

1. KNOCK AND GET APPROVAL TO COME IN
On a small ship we sail off the coast of Nova Scotia. We traverse a deep-water canyon, the continental slope, the abysmal plain. The canyon marine sanctuary is called The Gully, and its slopes are lined with fragile ancient cold-water coral.

Captain, are you there? Do you sense the continental drop-off as a princess does a pea?

2. DON'T MESS UP THE VIBES
My daughter writes the word vibes in a squiggly font to indicate fluidity. She double underlines it. The vibes are vulnerable, she says. In constant motion. In need of protection.

In The Gully, we spot a Northern Bottlenose whale, a creature of the deep. The whale breaches in a fit of triumph. Or maybe she is ailed by parasites. Does she feel threatened? Does she crave attention, admiration, light? She carries her young in her womb for 365 days. She spends most of her time in darkness. She holds her breath.

3. NO BEING LOUD OR ANNOYING TO ANYONE FOR THE SAKE OF THE VIBES

The traditional definition of caviar is roe that comes solely from fish of the sturgeon family. Unfertilized sturgeon eggs and salt create the delicacy. Baby Bottlenose whales are nursed for a year, after which time they are able to hunt and survive independently.

4. FIFTEEN MINUTES MAX UNLESS INVITED FOR LONGER

When my daughter was a year old, she was not a proficient hunter, nor was she an independent being. Money spent on her care could have purchased enough caviar to fill eleven and a half lifeboats.

The Northern Bottlenose whale is protected under the Marine Mammal Protection Act, which outlines the required response in the case of a stranding.

Captain, are you responsible for every body on this ship?

5. RESPECT ME (i.e. WHAT I SAY AND THE RULES)
The mating habits of the Northern Bottlenose whale are polygamous, and the females lack teeth. If my daughter lacked teeth, I'd have more money to buy more caviar. It's possible I could fill another lifeboat, or maybe a number of lifeboats, depending on the number of cavities my daughter develops over time. I struggle to remain abreast of her oral hygiene, as I am often procuring and preparing food, as she has not yet learned to be a proficient hunter and survive independently.

6. DON'T TOUCH ANYTHING WITHOUT ASKING (EXCEPTION: THE GROUND)
After a few days at sea, I acclimate to the pendulum rhythm and establish sea legs. For added security, I commit to memory the five steps of how to inflate a lifeboat.

7. GET OUT WHEN I SAY SO
Strandings of multiple marine mammals simultaneously within a defined area are referred to as mass strandings. Scientists use data from mass strandings to provide context for larger ocean health trends.

8. DON'T BREAK ANYTHING
– On lifeboat, locate and expose the shackle
– Ensure all lines are free of tangles and correctly positioned to avoid snagging
– Attach hook to shackle

– Pull out full length of line
– Give sharp tug to inflate lifeboat

Captain, are you there? How slippery is the deck today?

9. DON'T DIS MY BOOKS IN GENERAL OR HARRY
POTTER SPECIFICALLY
The ship is caught in rain, drizzle, and fog, and we collide
with something concrete. We begin to capsize, and women
and children are piled into lifeboats. There is a collective discombobulation because the lifeboats are full of caviar. This
is not the time for caviar, one woman says. This is ridiculous,
downright outrageous, others agree. It's a bloody mess.

Captain, are you there? The whistle on my life vest appears to
be broken. There is no sound. Captain?

10. DO NOT ENTER IF THE DOOR IS CLOSED
BECAUSE YOU WEREN'T RAISED BY ANIMALS AND
IF YOU WERE YOUR NAME WOULD BE MOWGLI
We are stranded.
    We are stranded with children, and the children are wet
and hungry. One has an earache, and the screams are beyond
the beyond. Captain?
            Captain?
        Are you there?
Captain?

With bare hands, the women empty the lifeboats of caviar. We dump the roe into the sea. We watch as pearls of luminescence disperse beyond the protected area, making their steady descent to the fragile slope of the abysmal plain.

LIFTED

In gymnastics, Dana was not the leader. That was Cheryl Ingram, whose handsprings had spunk. She arched from feet to hands to feet again and again then planted, arms raised, chest puffed like a pigeon. That Ingram girl's got spunk, Dana's mother said as they drove home after practice. Snow flurried in the Labrador night. Vanilla Ice on the radio: If there was a problem, yo, he'll solve it. He was the coolest. Dana's hands smelled of chalk and rubber and bare feet.

Cheryl Ingram's legs were sinew and muscles and ball joints perfectly aligned and limber and lean. Even her butt poking out of her leotard was muscular. She had a mean underbite that fixed her face in a scowl. Cheryl explained to Dana that her handsprings needed lift. It was all about timing, she said. You either have it, or you don't.

One day before practice Dana peed a little bit. She must have held it too long or maybe she was too cold from the three-minute walk between her mother's van and the gym. The pee made a dark stain on her leotard, and she hoped the others wouldn't notice. Gymnasts were upside down a lot though. It was all crotches and bottoms, soles and palms, pits, and arms.

They gathered, the team of five taking turns performing their floor routines. Provincials were in Newfoundland in two weeks.

"I smell . . . piss," Cheryl said. She crossed her arms and squinted as she surveyed the group of ten-year-old girls, who sniffed obediently.

Cheryl leaned into Dana. Dana could see the hair on her crossed arms. "Dana? You pissed yourself?" Cheryl's stare lowered to Dana's crotch. "You're fucking gross." She shook her head as if suffering on everyone's behalf, then glided onto the floor with the slick grace of a swan. Dana retreated behind the others and watched Cheryl's routine, which was majestic and stain free.

Dana's mind withdrew to Newfoundland, where she spent her summers. There, she picked bakeapple berries, sold them to tourists on the highway, then day-tripped with her mother to St. John's where she spent her berry money on school clothes at the Avalon Mall. The mall was more exciting than the moon. Her hometown in Labrador didn't have a mall. It didn't have McDonald's or stoplights or taxicabs, either. You had to take a plane or a ferry to see those things. In the summers, Dana and her parents filled coolers with Oreo cookies, Tang, ham sandwiches, celery, and peanut butter and lugged them onto the Sir Robert Bond ferry, where they set up in a four-berth cabin. When Dana sat on the top bunk, her head grazed the ceiling so her hair floated with static. Her bunk had a night-light that buzzed, and the walls creaked as they sailed for thirty-two hours from Goose Bay to Lewisporte, the intercom binging every time it announced the start of a movie or the sighting of an iceberg.

Last summer Dana had toured the Avalon Mall with her older cousin Judy and some of Judy's friends. Judy was thirteen, with friendship bracelets shielding both tanned arms. A streak of blue garnished her blonde hair. She wore gold feather earrings, tight ripped jeans, and studded leather ankle boots. Everyone wanted to be her friend. A group of boys slumped at a table in the food court, and one of them hollered at Judy. She glanced, smiled, and kept walking, her feather earrings tick-tocking above her neck.

The 'It Store' was new and electric and like nothing Dana had ever seen. It was bursting with toys and noise and games and candy and lights, and Dana thought of her home, her street, her school in Labrador, and couldn't understand how those places existed at the same time as this store. Even the floor was out-of-this-world blue carpet speckled with comets and moons and stars. Nothing was recognizable, not even the music, which seemed to wobble and click. Judy gave her the tour as if the place belonged to her. One wall was made entirely of Rubik's Cubes. Lite-Brite screens lined another wall with pixilated clowns and sailboats and Pac-Man. Balloons floated around an enormous pillar of candy powder with eight dispensers, each containing a different flavour. Green apple blast, blue cotton candy, dragon fruit. You could combine the flavours to make a rainbow. Judy led them to the back of the store, where the lights were dim, and everything had breasts. Mugs with breasts, slippers with breasts, T-shirts and aprons with breasts. Ruby nipples pointed in every direction. Judy put on a breast hat and turned it sideways. One of Judy's friends choked on her candy powder, laughing, coughing up green apple blast slime, wiping her face with her sleeve.

"You need adult supervision back there," a clerk barked from behind the counter.

At the front of the store there was a display piled with stuffed toys. Judy casually placed them into sex positions. Giraffes humping frogs, hippos humping elephants, a monkey groping a moose. Her friends cowered, giggled, squeezed candy powder into their mouths, and when Judy twirled on her heel and left the store, they followed.

. . . .

During the final week before provincials, the coaches took videos of the girls' routines. In the front foyer of the Labrador Rec Centre, Cheryl sat inches from the TV screen, remote clutched in her hand, replaying sections of her routine. Dana straddled on the floor, stretching her hamstrings.

"Didn't think my split leap hit one-eighty, but it totally did." Cheryl paused the video as she crested the leap.

"Awesome line, Cheryl," Tracy said from a half-lotus position on the floor. Emily sat behind her, massaging her shoulders.

"Dana, look at your humpback. I can't stop looking at it." Dana straightened. "What?"

Cheryl paused the video, zooming in on Dana, who stood near the uneven bars, cradling her elbows. She slumped forward, slightly rounding her back.

"Our very own humpback. *Humpback of Notre Dana*," Cheryl jeered, stooping.

Emily smiled and focussed on Tracy's shoulders. Tracy stared at the floor.

"And why do you always hold your elbows? You look like a retard."

Still stooped, Cheryl held her own elbows, rocked, grunted, and snorted, forcing her top teeth over her bottom lip.

"Cheryl, settle down. Not cool," Tracy said, keeping her eyes on the floor between her legs.

"Cool? I don't give two shits about cool. Poise is crazy important. *Retard* here is going to drag down our score with her fucking humpback."

"I won't slouch at Provincials, Cheryl. It's just . . . I was relaxing." She pretended to stretch her other hamstring.

"You of all people should not be relaxing. Your back extension sucks. Why are you even on this team?" Cheryl threw the remote control on the floor near Dana. The battery shot out, ricocheted, and hit Dana's bent knee. Jittery, Dana picked up the battery and replaced it in the remote. Her mouth and throat, dry as salt.

"And what on earth is on your arms? Zits? Do you even wash?"

Every winter, prickly red pimples appeared on the underside of Dana's arms. She rooted in her bag for her sweatshirt and pulled it over her head as Cheryl stomped out of the room. They didn't watch the rest of the video. Dana was glad of it. She had fumbled her first tumbling pass and tripped during her full turn.

....

The weekend of Provincials arrived, and the plane landed in St. John's at nine-thirty in the morning. They registered at the gym. Opening Ceremonies started at six p.m., which meant a full day at the Avalon Mall.

Dana pictured herself leading her team around the mall. She'd show them the food court. She'd recommend Teen Burgers at A&W, the frozen glass of slushy root beer. She would present the 'It Store,' its candy, its carpet, its breasts. She would place the stuffed toys in sex positions. She'd show them that it was no big deal for her. She'd remember to shrug. Dana would show them that she was all about having fun in the big city.

In the mall, Cheryl was on a mission. There was a hot tub in their hotel, and she had forgotten her swimsuit. She would meet them at A&W.

The girls ordered their burgers and fries and were just finishing as Cheryl arrived and plopped a bag in the middle of their table. She leaned on the bag as if she were holding down a wild beast.

"I changed the price tag on this swimsuit. Look!" She flaunted a shimmering blue and lime-green swimsuit. Its price tag, $9.99. "It was actually $29.99."

"You shoplifted, Cheryl? Seriously?" Tracy dug in her chin, repulsed. The others exchanged wide-eyed glances.

"Lighten up, Tracy. It's just a swimsuit," Cheryl said as she straightened and frowned at the bag.

"It's really no big deal, Tracy," Dana said. "It was probably going on sale anyway."

"It's a Speedo, you idiot," Cheryl said. "Speedos don't go on sale. It's a top-of-the-line competitive swimsuit." She glared at Dana and snatched her bag off the table.

Dana's hands trembled. "Don't call me that."

"What are you going to do? Lift your leg and piss on me?" The others laughed and Dana flushed. She got up and walked away, hoping that at least one of the girls would follow, but none of them did.

As Dana walked through the mall, she noticed a mannequin in a storefront with spiked hair and feathered earrings.

She entered and gazed at the clothing, thinking of Cheryl's nasty face, her back handsprings, her hairy arms. Her hands stopped shaking as she sifted through the clothing. Feathers and fringes and spikes. This must be the style for city girls. Judy probably shops here. She should call Judy. No one would laugh at Judy. Dana grabbed an armful of feathery, fringed, spiky items.

In the fitting room she tried on the new clothes. The clothing looked edgy on her scrawny frame as she posed, puckered her lips, and raised a shoulder in the mirror. She was a city girl, just like that. Her spirits lifted. A pink and silver cashmere sweater was the softest and most luxurious thing she had ever touched. It draped her shoulders and even gave shape to her flat chest. All of a sudden, she had little curved breasts. She angled the sweater off one shoulder. The fitting room lights caught the silver and sparkled. She stared at herself as though this vision might disappear at any moment.

Dana counted her money and looked at the price tags and made her piles of yeses, nos, and maybes, the way her mother had taught her on their summer shopping days. The cost of the sweater exceeded the entire amount of her spending money. She tried it on again. Breasts. She sat on the floor of the fitting room.

Dana zipped her coat up to her chin, careful not to hitch the pink and silver wool. She kept both hands on her wallet, holding it tightly to stop her hands from shaking as she paid for the other items. Her heart pounded as she exited the store. Nothing beeped. The sweater was hers. She was a city girl, and she had breasts.

As she walked through the mall, she removed her coat and tucked it into her shopping bag. The sweater was loose and light, and she felt a breeze on her midriff. She focussed on her posture and swung her shopping bag like a pendulum. Leather-studded boots with heels would *make* this outfit, she thought. A click-clack to let people know that she has arrived. A group of boys walked in her direction. She was sure that their eyes lingered, and she resisted the urge to make eye contact as they passed. They'd look back at her, nudge each other. Perhaps they'd make a comment about her breasts. She found her team outside the movie theatre; Emily and Cheryl were competing to see who could hold a standing split the longest.

"Wow! Nice sweater, Dana!" Tracy pet the wool like it was a lamb.

"How much?" Cheryl snapped.

"Free." Dana put her hands on her hips. "Lifted."

"No you didn't." Cheryl moved closer, examining the sweater.

Tracy was shaking her head. "You guys are gonna get us sent home."

"We're not stupid, Tracy," Cheryl said. "You don't take stuff that has detectors on it." Cheryl touched the sweater, rubbing the wool between her fingers.

"Dana, bring it back. Tell them you forgot or something," Emily said, scanning the others for allies.

Dana considered this. She had taken so many items into the fitting room. She could say it was an accident. Or she could go back and admit what she did. Maybe they'd let her off this once, praise her for fessing up.

"The sweater looks awesome, Dana," Cheryl said. "It's a perfect fit for you." Cheryl's face softened as she linked arms with Dana. The two of them slipped seamlessly away from the group.

Later, Cheryl and Dana walked out of a shoe store with matching black heeled boots that had leather fringes around the ankles. The heels clicked on the tile floor as alarms sounded and lights beamed and flashed. The cashier swept them to the back of the store as she ordered a call for security.

"Boots off. Now!" The cashier was a petite woman with big hair and cigarette-stained fingers. As she emptied their bags, her eyebrows lifted making rows of wrinkles across her forehead that reminded Dana of quicksand. The girls' old running sneakers poked out of the pile of sparkling, fringed, stolen clothing that was now strewn over the grey carpet. They stood barefoot. Cheryl started to weep.

The security guards' office was in the basement of the mall. On the desk, an ashtray overflowed with cigarette butts and foil gum wrappers and fresh new ashes from the cigarette the guard held between his teeth. Cheryl sat at another desk with another guard, crying, her body coiled and retching. She pointed in Dana's direction and gestured to her shirt. She was telling them about the sweater. The air, stale and heavy, reeked of cigarettes and damp concrete. Dana felt a hot wave of nausea as the sweater clung to the sweat on her back. She looked down, and in the dull light, the silver in her sweater appeared grey. The bits that made it sparkle, Dana could see, were thin slivers of foil, not unlike the foil in the ashtray. The slivers made her itch, and the tag scraped the back of her neck. Cheryl's sobs morphed into a raspy rhythm that sounded like someone sweeping.

In a swift overhead manoeuvre, Dana peeled the sweater from her body and carefully placed it on the guard's desk. The sobbing ceased. The guard lowered his cigarette, blinking turtle-like at Dana in her sports bra, minding her posture. Through the arched swarm of smoke, Dana barely recognized Cheryl, her outline concave and wilted, and the only sound was the cackle of springs in the chairs beneath the feather-weight of their bodies.

HALF-LIFE

1.

Anik was my uncle. He was named after the satellite that brought TV to the Canadian North. I shared a birthday with him, and every September he arrived at our house in Goose Bay, Labrador, to celebrate.

In the winter months, Anik travelled to warm and arid places. He sent postcards of sand dunes and red rock spires against vibrant blue skies. I later learned that he wintered in Moab, Utah, where he had friends (lovers), who gave him a home if he cooked and cleaned and tended the garden. He also ran marathons all over the world. At our house he made salsas and fried bread called sopaipillas that left me feeling snug and creaturely.

During his visits, I was given permission to stay up late, sometimes well past midnight, to watch the northern lights.

He showed me how to whistle the auroras into bloom. He shared his extensive knowledge of famous Earth-grazing meteors and recited "The Cremation of Sam McGee" by heart. It was on one of these nights that Anik told me he was a depressive. "I'm a depressive," he said, as blackflies feasted on the nape of his neck. He struggled most in the fall of the year and said that for him, the decay of autumn prompted a giant tipping into deep sorrow. I had not imagined that someone like Anik could experience deep sorrow. He had always seemed so light and playful. I had not imagined deep sorrow. I was relieved that night, when he shifted the subject to the phenomenon of the blue light spiral that had appeared in the sky above Tromsø, Norway. People thought it was a UFO sighting, but it turned out to be a Russian ballistic missile, a failed launch from a nuclear submarine in the White Sea.

On my tenth birthday, Anik turned twenty-seven, and he arrived with an upright hammock. He installed it high up in a birch tree in our backyard and hammered pieces of board to the trunk for steps. I carried my dolls up there, my books, my journal, my threads of plastic for weaving friendship bracelets. When it rained, I took my umbrella up to my hammock and pretended to be a planet. Other years, Anik brought a zipline, a trick scooter, a remote-control plane. He went all out when he played, one time even fracturing his elbow. His gifts had a curious way of making the two of us central, and my love for him became intricate. Our connection evolved exponentially. He sent postcards every few months, mostly news of his marathons, the progress of his gardens, the discovery of an ocean on one of Saturn's moons. Anik's postcards from the outside world shepherded me through girlhood.

While staying at our house, Anik went for runs before dawn, and then joined me for breakfast and walked me to school. His sweaty smell was oniony. It made me imagine his insides — his hip bones, the cartilage inside his ear. He had a lean sinewy body, and his baby toenails were black. He liked to draw attention to them, calling them his nasties. Anik crossed his legs when seated, his foot bobbing as if conducting a symphony, silently directing phrases.

There were times when Anik let me accompany him during his hill workouts at the old NORAD radar station. He sprinted up the gravel incline, turned around, jogged casually down the slope, and sprinted up again. As he did this, I wandered around the remains of the site, which was called Pinetree. All that remained of the radar station were two squat cubic buildings, and at the top of the hill, a giant white sphere on a metal tower. At the time, I knew nothing of early warning radar systems. The Pinetree Line station had been built to detect Soviet bombers during the Cold War, but to me, the peculiar structure might have been a Christmas parade float, or a prop abandoned by a circus troop that ventured to Labrador only to fold beneath the bitter cold. Shrubs and alders had begun their takeover of the site, and beyond the creeping alders, dense forest extended down the sandy valley to the Churchill River and the Mealy Mountains, making the spherical structure on the hill an incongruent pendant in the middle of The Big Land; a symbol of remoteness perched on the northern edge of a continent, able to endure extreme cold, yet sensitive to the presence of oppressive forces.

When I was a girl, I wasn't curious about Anik's family. I never met his partner or his son, who had been born severely disabled. Once, Anik was playing tag with me, and I tripped and smashed my face into the corner of the living room wall. My mother held me in her arms, pressed a bag of ice to my cheek, and told Anik he should be with his own family. That was it — my only link to Anik's family world. He sat still as I tick-tocked in my mother's arms, acquiescent about what Mom had said, reacting more like a pet than a grown-up, but now I see that Anik had his own quiet way of orbiting shame and disquiet.

The autumn I turned sixteen, Anik turned thirty-three. He didn't visit. He emailed my mother to say he was unwell. It came as a shock that Anik had access to email, because he consistently held that social media and online forms of posturing eroded an authentic sense of self. On my birthday, a package arrived with a postcard and a wooden box full of coins from all over the world. The postcard was in Anik's handwriting, but it wasn't like his other postcards; it was just a sentence, really: *Anik Blake passed peacefully away in Tromsø, Norway, surrounded by friends and magnificent northern lights.*

This September I will exceed Anik in age. It feels to me like an unsolvable riddle.

2.

Anik was my aunt. She was named after the satellite that brought TV to the Canadian North. I shared a birthday with her, and every September she arrived at our house in Goose Bay to celebrate.

In the winter months, Anik travelled to warm and arid places. She sent postcards of sand dunes and red rock spires against vibrant blue skies. I later learned that she wintered in Moab, Utah, where she had friends (lovers), who gave her a home if she cooked and cleaned and tended the garden. She also ran marathons all over the world. At our house she made salsas and fried bread called sopaipillas that left me feeling snug and creaturely.

It was the year I turned thirteen that Anik took me to the sandhill on the back of the military base to try out the remote-control plane she'd bought for my birthday. It started to pour, so we found shelter inside some abandoned military barracks. Heavy ropes dangled from the ceiling, and we pushed desks and shelves together, climbed on top of them and jumped, swinging from the suspended ropes. We soared across the vacant dusty room as sun glinted through mouldy windows. Anik was mid-swing when one of the ropes gave way, crashing her to the floor. She let me take the wheel as we drove to the hospital. There, she expressed concern to the nurses about missing her morning runs and slipping into depression. She struggled in the fall of the year, she said. "A giant tipping into deep sorrow." It surprised me to hear her talk about sorrow like that. She didn't seem sad to me, just thoughtful and intimate. Anik couldn't touch her fingertips to her shoulder or straighten her arm without pain, so they sent her for an x-ray, and as we looked at the fractured elbow, I imagined Anik's skeletal frame radiating light beneath her skin.

Anik sent postcards every few months, mostly news of her marathons, the progress of her gardens, the discovery of an ocean on one of Saturn's moons. She sent a postcard from Tromsø, Norway, where she ran a marathon every June. It was her favourite marathon because it took place during perpetual sunlight. Anik's postcards from the outside world shepherded me through girlhood. I kept them in my journal, often reading through them while relaxing in my hammock.

During her visits to Goose Bay, Anik walked me to school in the mornings. One day, Joey Broomfield's two Rottweilers barrelled into the street, their chests slick and muscular. They barked violently, their mouths quivering over greasy teeth. Anik wore running shorts, and I was terrified that the dogs would rip into her bare legs. She kept walking though. She remained calm as the dogs growled, even as one of them lunged at a fuzzy keychain dangling from my backpack. That morning Anik used the word neutral to describe how we could escape from the dogs. It was the first time I had thought about the word neutral. It was important, she said, to keep walking without showing fear or aggression. Be neutral and the dogs will lose interest. Anik spoke to me as if I were an adult, and when I told her that Joey Broomfield was the town dogcatcher, that his job was to capture stray dogs, that he had captured my dog, Raz, twice, and we had paid a fine, she said it was ironic — another new word that seemed revelatory at the time.

There were times when Anik let me accompany her during her hill workouts at the old NORAD radar station. She sprinted up the gravel incline, turned around, jogged casually down the slope, and sprinted up again. As she did this, I wandered around the remains of the site, which was called Pinetree. All that remained of the radar station were two squat cubic buildings, and at the top of the hill, a giant white sphere on a metal tower. At the time, I knew nothing of these early warning radar systems. I had no idea that they'd been built during the Cold War, perched on the edge of a continent, able to endure extreme cold, and sensitive to the presence of oppressive forces. Anik showed me an old bunker that had been used to store American nuclear armaments in the 1950s. A concrete half-octagon structure with a large vehicular door. It got her talking about instability of plutonium, excess of internal energy and radioactivity. "Their internal imbalance causes them to self-destruct and decay and emit radiation." She was fascinated by the concept of half-life. Trees had grown up all around the bunker, giving it a burrowed perspective, and as we climbed on top of it, she told me about Cory, a skateboarder military kid from Germany, skinny/tall/long hair/baggy khaki pants. In high school they came here to make out. "This was our spot," she said. "My first hickey, on top of a nuclear bunker."

When I was a girl, I wasn't curious about Anik's family. I never met her partner or her son, who had been born severely disabled. Once, Anik was playing tag with me, and I tripped and smashed my face into the corner of the living room wall. My mother held me in her arms, pressed a bag of ice to my cheek, and told Anik she should be with her own family. That was it — my only link to Anik's family world. She sat still as I tick-tocked in my mother's arms, acquiescent about what Mom had said, reacting more like a pet than a grown-up, but now I see that Anik had her own quiet way of orbiting shame and disquiet.

The autumn I turned sixteen, Anik turned thirty-three. She didn't visit. She emailed my mother to say she was unwell. It came as a shock that Anik had access to email because she consistently held that social media and online forms of posturing eroded an authentic sense of self. On my birthday, a package arrived with a postcard and a wooden box full of coins from all over the world. The postcard was in Anik's handwriting, but it wasn't like her other postcards; it was just a sentence, really: *Anik Blake passed peacefully away in Tromsø, Norway, surrounded by friends and magnificent northern lights.*

This September I will exceed Anik in age.

3.

An unsolvable riddle, in retrograde, Anik will start to be younger than me. Anik will continue to surface between the paragraphs of my days, appearing as if on a radar, in particular scenes of remoteness — the sheen of a glass building at night, the parallel shadows of power lines on pavement, a lone seagull in an empty parking lot. Anik will reside in every earthquake, in every tropical storm and flood and wildfire, and as autumn approaches I will tune in to the infinite possibility of dormant forces. I'll stay awake after dark to watch the sky radiate with light.

CHRISTMAS CARD FOR THE WIN

¿Por qué están ustedes sorprendidos?
TAP TO SPEAK ¿Por qué están ustedes sorprendidos?
Nice! Meaning: Why are you surprised?

Gilles can feel his grumpiness lift like an early morning fog. He would prefer not to make this four-hour road trip to set up his tripod in front of a giant rooster, but admits that the ritual has its comforts. The drive is scenic (Burnt Lands Provincial Park), ironic (Sinders Bridal House), full of sameness (Notre Dame Catholic School), and sleepiness (Art's Mini-sheds) that make him feel at once wholesome and innovative. Despite the windy November day, his mood is buoyant as he drives. Stephen and Sophia sit in the back seat with their individual playlists. They are less than an hour into their annual road trip to Sonny the Rooster, who has been the background feature of their Christmas card for three years now. Linda's idea of course. She is a wizard in the curation of such things. A hoot and a half.

Linda is in the passenger seat with her sock feet on the dash, a habit Gilles discourages because of the strain this posture will put on her lumbar spine. Her low back pain stems from having two c-sections in two years, yet there she is, curled over her iPad like a gremlin, bingdonging through Duolingo Spanish, steadfast as ever.

> *Denada*
> *You missed a space. De_Nada.*
> *Translation: You are welcome.*

Linda imagines the front of her brain flooding with dopamine as she advances into eighth place in the Duolingo diamond league. Top ten finishers make it into the Promotion Zone. She thinks for a moment of the makeshift puppet show from nursing school five hundred years ago when Dr. Mike — or was it Dr. Matt? — glued cardboard brains to popsicle-stick spinal cords to illustrate the activities of the central nervous system when one is presented with a reward. Earlier this morning she received the Sharpshooter award for completing twenty lessons with no mistakes. She has a sixty-three-day streak. A row of badges from the leagues through which she has advanced illuminate the top of her screen. Bronze, silver, gold, sapphire, ruby, emerald, amethyst, pearl, obsidian, and diamond. A rainbow of progress that is having its way with her neurotransmitters. One of the app's cartoon characters, Junior, jumps and throws his arms in the air, vibrating as if he might explode with happiness. Another character, Nadira, sports a purple asymmetrical bob and slow claps whenever Linda gets things right. Cómo te llamas? Mi nombre es Linda. Mucho gusto.

They pass through the suburbs—carbon-copy beige and grey accordion-like houses. She can trick herself in the suburbs. She can pretend she's in any number of places. Any number of the places she has lived in since marrying Gilles and the army. This suburb in particular, the width of its streets, the style of its fences, the skinny trees, is remarkably like Kingston, and even Petawawa, if the trees were more mature. Who would have thought that a military life, with all its upheaval, could have so much monotony? She remembers when she first spotted Sonny the Rooster perched atop his horn of plenty. It was during their move from Winnipeg to Ottawa three years ago. Or was it two years ago? Immediately she knew Sonny would be memorable. In the outskirts of Ottawa now, the fields are vast and rolling, ploughed in parallel lines that flash before her. Oh, there's that farmhouse. A cross-stitch-worthy stone build with pale blue trim. Adjacent, in a sprawling junkyard, a pod camper sits slant, its windows broken, its door removed. The farmhouse is smart against the bloat of the junkyard. Objects at rest long enough to create a savage sort of harmony. It occurs to her that this is their last Sonny the Rooster road trip because they are posted to Colorado Springs this coming July. Her giddiness wanes into that vacant sense of being between two places. A menacing, tumbleweed mood that infiltrates the months before a military move. She can anticipate the lack of bearings she will have in a new city. It used to be an adventure, but now she imagines the brain synapses that will burn out as she bumbles through the maze of another new place.

It's been three years in Ottawa, she figures out gradually. Three years. Linda feels stretched like plastic wrap across the surface of the city, instead of existing as a meaningful element within it. Sonny the Rooster, at least, offers a sort of tradition, a waypoint that doesn't blend in with its surroundings. A short-lived feeling of intense happiness. Emocionado, meaning moved by emotion. Not to be mistaken with excitado, which means sexually aroused or horny.

"Duo says I'm crushing it," she says.

"You're still in the Promotion Zone?" Gilles asks, keeping his eyes on the road.

"Eighth place, with twenty-three minutes to go."

"How far are you from first place?"

"Oh, God, like over three thousand xp," Linda says. "Pointless to even go for it. Pointless. Jaquie42 has 4186 xp. I mean, she must never do anything else." She looks up briefly. "I do admire her commitment though."

Tap the matching pairs: table — mesa; boy — niño; or — o;
cheap — barato.
BING DONG Correct!

"Have you connected with this Jaquie42?" Gilles asks. "Can you do that?"

"No. It's just random people. They change every week."

Type what you hear.
¿Tu estás también sorprendido, Pedro?
BING DONG Nicely done!
Translation: You are also surprised, Pedro?

"Did you know you can buy coffins at Costco?" Linda asks.

"I did not know this."

From the driver's seat, Gilles glances at Linda. He desperately wishes she would stop competing with random people on the internet and maybe spend these hours researching Colorado. It is so windy, he has to grip the wheel with both hands and can feel a dull ache in his forearms. Lengthy road trips such as this one typically gives them the time and enclosed vehicular space to — *a veces tú te levantas cansada.* *BING DONG* — develop upcoming family plans, vacations, etcetera. He would like to discuss the move, start organizing themselves. Schools? Neighbourhoods? Family physician? Dentist? Nearest airport? Swim lessons for Stephen? Dance

for Sophia? — *El niño nunca se levanta a las siete los sábados.*
BING DONG — Driver's licences? Insurance? Vaccinations?
Why hasn't she started looking into rental houses yet? Just
this week he noticed a three-jar package of natural peanut
butter from Costco. Seems like poor form, given that they
will be moving in six months. Is she no longer on board with
the move? She had expressed enthusiasm when he'd first men-
tioned Colorado. He would almost definitely get a promotion
to Major as a result of his job there — *¿Te duchas la mañana o
la noche? BING DONG.*

Gilles reaches into the side compartment for a clear plastic
container that holds balls of wax. He rolls one between his
fingers and presses it into his right ear. Linda notices.

"Situational awareness much?" she says, returning her gaze
to her iPad.

"My situational awareness is intact. These take the edge off
the bings of your second language training."

"Duo thinks I'm amazing," Linda says. "According to Duo,
my hard work is paying off."

Gilles winks at Linda while pushing the ball of wax deeper
into his ear cavity. He feels a sense of triumph as the decibels
around him relent into vague underwater tones. He places his
hand on her thigh, and she touches the back of his neck for a
moment, a light, placating rub before she returns to her iPad.
He loves it when she touches his neck like that.

Winnipeg. Was it four or five years ago? Stephen was in kindergarten. So flippin' cute. Gilles glances in the rear-view to see Stephen racing against himself on his Rubik's Cube for which he has memorized the algorithms. He is likely listening to NF or Chance the Rapper. Thirteen already. How? And Sophia, folding and linking squares of origami paper into transforming ninja stars. Sophia is like Gilles. Everyone says it, and it delights and worries him in equal measure. She is almost too even-keeled for eleven. A shape-shifter. A people pleaser. Calm and steady until her reserve expires. Gilles can sense the weariness that exists beneath her stoic front, and it gnaws at him. But what was he just thinking? Winnipeg. Linda found that little house in an older neighbourhood, dense with trees, a stone's throw from a basement wine bar where they had double-date nights with another military couple, Carrie and Martin. Then there was their little house in Kingston, before kids. Linda had found a brick house on Belvedere Street with maroon velvet wallpaper. They joined a swing dance club. Met up with her nursing friends at Wallace Hall to watch vintage swing videos and dance. Seems like another lifetime. Every new place they live in is sort of like a lifetime.

When Gilles was deployed to the radar station in Clear, Alaska, Linda decided to take the kids to Newfoundland for the year. It was a place she'd always wanted to visit, she'd said. What a rash move. A recipe for burnout. Linda with a newborn and a two-year-old, on her own in a new place. But there was no stopping her; she was like high tide. She found a furnished apartment on York Street just minutes from the harbour front. She met her neighbours while shovelling herself out of a snow drift. They were musicians with a five-year-old. They hung out, drank tea, made Wikki Stix eyeglasses, paper bag monster puppets, clothespin dragonflies, fuzzball bookmarks. They lit sparklers after dark and ran around in the snowy street with winter coats unzipped and cape-like.

The flow of pictures from York Street kept Gilles afloat that year. He had almost no human contact in Alaska. He worked night shifts, only seeing the sun every eight days when he had four days off that he spent mostly alone and always depressed. He was able to work out every day, which made him almost content with his body, but he'd never felt so hollow. With the downtime, he might have improved his French language profile, or completed DP4 and 5 of Leader Development which would have won him three PD points on his annual PER, nudging him closer to a promotion. He didn't do any of those things. He watched *Game of Thrones* and played *Legend of Zelda*. What a waste. He'll never have that kind of time again. He missed them though, Linda and the kids and their infinite needs. He'd wake from sleep convinced he was dying.

"Dad, the cows are eating in the same field as those giant electrical towers," Stephen says as Gilles turns on the radio to a punchy rap of someone calling a phone like they're locked up. He switches the station quickly and it's the same song—planes and fuckin' helicopters. He turns the radio off.

"It's a perfectly good place for the cows, Stephen."

BING DONG

"Mom, don't you think it's weird? The cows?"

"Stephen! Leave your mother alone."

Linda looks over her shoulder. "Sorry, what hon?"

"The field with the cows and the big electrical towers."

"What field, hon?"

"It's gone. We passed it."

Linda checks her leaderboard. She's moved into sixth place with sixteen minutes to go. The ten names inside the Promotion Zone are flashing. She has won ten lingots.

> *How do you say pen?*
> *Bolígrafo*
> *BING DONG Good job!*

Gilles breathes in, exhales dramatically, putting his chest and shoulders into it.

"Would you like me to drive?" Linda asks.

"No."

"Your mood shift is palpable and in poor taste."

"That's rich. I'm impressed at your ability to sense my mood, what with your current competitive streak."

"Fair, but still . . . and yes, I have a sixty-three-day streak, and also you are being—" she pauses, searching, "niggling. You are niggling." She makes a face, scrunchy nose, sourpuss.

"Thank goodness," Gilles says, looking straight ahead, two hands on the wheel.

"Yes, thank goodness."

Linda is being generous with niggling. Gilles is a killjoy. His body language is at odds with his words. It is clear he didn't want to come on this road trip. Last night she poured him a glass of wine, one of their favourites, and he had made no comment. No swirl swirl, plunge of the nose and contemplation: "Notes of boot. Notes of boot when said boot is first removed from box . . . at Winners," like he had done that time in Winnipeg with Marty and Carrie. She had laughed so hard in that delightfully cavernous wine bar. Last night though, Gilles was glossy-eyed as Stephen went on and on and on about *Pixel Car Racer* mode, upshift, burnout, nitro clutch, in-game cash, drivetrain. Gilles focussed on chewing his food. Gulped his wine. Retreated into hibernation deep within his brain cave.

Maybe he's depressed, she thinks. Maybe it's the pandemic. Oddly, the pandemic has hardly altered her existence. She doesn't miss large family or social gatherings, because they haven't been a part of her life for years. Isolation feels like home. Her nuclear family. Her island existence.

After supper last night, she watered her plants, which have become lush and jungle-like over the past three years. They overflow their pots and lean into the sun. Gilles's suppertime silence had grated on her, but as she cleared away dead foliage and loosened tangles, her irritation also loosened. Her plants demanded so little of her.

> *Which of these is the husband?*
> *El esposo*
> *BING DONG Excellent!*

Linda walked out on her first husband after only nine months of marriage. An old hockey injury left him with a jaw that clicked, and when he chewed his food he sounded like a starving, hiccupping beast. He refused jaw surgery and elected to live with the misalignment, ignoring the clicks. Often, at the crest of a yawn, his jaw locked, painfully out of joint, forcing him to manually realign his face. Linda's first husband did not communicate with words but with clicks and grunts, groans, sniffles, sighs, stormy exhales.

Linda knew that Gilles was a keeper the first time she saw him naked. It wasn't the sex. Sex was tame — awkward even. No, it was the folds in his skin that sealed their future together. Gilles and two of his army friends had participated in an extreme weight-loss challenge and he'd shed seventy-five pounds in less than six months. Excess skin draped like molten layers with a texture of something shivering. When he removed his shirt, the acoustics of the room shifted. He became shy, he cradled his core, and Linda felt lighthearted and dreamy. Somehow, she knew that it was these particular folds that gave Gilles the ability to ward off her particular chaos.

She leans over and kisses Gilles's cheek, shuts her iPad and places her hand on his lap. He cups his hand over hers.

"Giving up on your leaderboard?"

"Pacing myself."

Gilles feels himself relax. Just like that. All Linda has to do is touch him like that. She can be so callous and closed. Cold. She can say something like, Oh Gilles, you are such a prude, you are eroding my very soul, who cares Gilles, gawd, why are you so rigid? and it upsets him, and most times makes him spiral into his own hell in which he considers his bulging stomach. His belt at this moment cuts into him as his stomach piles over it. The belt and his jeans will indent a track across his skin that will be numb and itchy when he removes his clothes tonight, quietly, so as not to disturb Linda. She will be sleeping soundly, having taken anti-inflammatories for the back pain that will have set in after eight hours in a car with such a gremlin-like posture. He will try his best not to disturb her, but will secretly hope, as he hopes every night, that she will wake and reach an arm over to his side of the bed, and that this reaching arm will lead to slow, hushed sex and intense eye contact that ends in naked spooning. It's been so long, and his stomach — excessive travelling in the last two years has derailed his workout routine and he's heavier than ever, but all she has to do is touch him like that. It's like a reset. Linda removes her hand from his lap and opens her iPad.

"Ninth place!" she shrieks. "This week's leaderboard is wolfish!"

Gilles will never forget the conversation they had on their very first date. It was in Edmonton. Linda explained that a red flag for her was an inability to articulate emotion. Gilles thought he would faint with happiness; he was a sentimentalist. A few weeks following their first date, something locked into place when they saw each other at a Mexican eatery. They hadn't planned to meet that day. He had not expected to see her but had been thinking of her constantly since the Sunday prior when they'd had sex for the first time. He had been thinking about her solid body, her broad shoulders, the folksy shape of her un-manicured fingernails. She had been astonishingly alert and attentive during sex. All he wanted was to be near her, to sink his teeth into her, gentle bites. When she appeared in the Mexican eatery where he was having lunch with his boss, Major Lake, and his boss's boss, Colonel Haire, he thought his mind had conjured her. She was alone and wearing plum-coloured corduroy pants. Surprised to see him, she waved, bouncy as she approached his table. Gilles rose to greet her and when she neared him, she did an awkward kung-fu kick. There was no contact (it was an air kick), but yet, he ducked his head playfully, held his fists below his chin. A back and forth of jerky sparring between them, and he was overcome with animated feelings. He did not introduce her to Major Lake and Colonel Haire because he forgot they were there. He could only think of the way she guarded her face with her fists. That kick.

A whiff of something vile fills the car. Something off. Like the inside of a plastic container that's stored pickled things, but even more putrid. A yeasty, sourdough smell. Roadkill? Linda doesn't seem to notice. Or maybe, was it her? What is going on there? She has often expressed that she can't help the gas. That it's all linked to her hormonal journey. Nasty. Truly.

"Stephen! Gross," Sophia yells from the back seat. "Put your shoes back on, Stephen."

Stephen sits with his leg crossed over his thigh, figure four, rancid foot bobbing.

"Ugh . . . whatever, Sophia. What—ever."

"Like . . ." Sophia scooches away from him in the back seat. "They smell like fish. Ugh. I'm gonna puke."

"*I'm gonna puke,*" Stephen mocks. "Unbelievable." He opens his window, and the inside of the car is blasted with wind as squares of paper flit like a frenzy of winged insects.

"MY ORIGAMI! STEPHEN! CLOSE THE WINDOW!"
Sophia screams. "STEPHEN!"

"STEPHEN, CLOSE THE WINDOW! NOW!" Gilles
yells over the wind, glaring into the rear-view. "LINDA?
COULD YOU HANDLE THIS PLEASE?"

Linda doesn't look up from her iPad.

Stephen closes the window. Silence.

BING DONG

"I have two minutes left," Linda says.

"I am driving."

"Not a crisis, Gilles. Not a crisis," she says, tapping her
iPad.

It is beyond irritating to Gilles when she does this. Her
inner charge nurse capability. You haven't been a nurse in over
a decade, he wants to yell. You are an expired nurse. Let it be,
Gilles, she'll say. Not a crisis, Gilles, and it irks him, and there
she is, look at her, calm, collected, but sometimes, you know
what? She's lazy. She is lazy. I could be calm, he thinks, and
chill. I could be calm and chill if my only priority were beat-
ing out this week's Duolingo diamond league.

This week, for example, on top of his normal workload,
he completed the Complex Project and Procurement Leadership: Soft Systems Methodology — a course required for his
promotion. Awake until after two a.m. on Wednesday and
Thursday, answering time-sensitive emails about the Maritime
Patrol project for sonars and sonobuoys. And what's her

priority? Scoring experience points on Duolingo. He grinds his teeth.

"Stephen, Sophia," he says now, masking irritation with incisiveness. "I want you to start looking at extracurricular activities in Colorado Springs."

"No, thank you," Sophia says sweetly.

"Seriously?" Stephen says. "You don't want to move to Colorado? After two weeks there, your body will have more red blood cells because of the altitude. Did you know that?"

"I don't want to leave my friends," Sophia says. "I have friends, Stephen."

"I have friends," Stephen says.

"No, you don't."

"I do."

"Nope."

"I have friends, Sophia," Stephen says, annoyed. "Logan." He pauses. "Philip is a good friend."

"Logan?" Sophia folds a square of star-patterned paper. "Logan didn't even invite you to his Laser Tag birthday party, and Phil is a ghost. He is never even in school."

"His parents only let him invite six people," Stephen says. "Whatever, Sophia." He cycles a row of his Rubik's Cube. "Your five hundred BFFs will forget you in two seconds. You'll see."

Translate this sentence.
Linda, why do you feel sad?
¿Linda por qué te sientes triste?
BING DONG Nicely done!

The Duolingo bear cartoon character has a unibrow and a blue scarf and is unflinching in this section on emotions. Linda would like to joke about this with Gilles but can sense that he is in a mood. This is how it would go down: Look at this, hon, Duolingo is asking me why I feel sad. And Gilles would say, hmm, capping the conversation. Utter killjoy.

Does she feel sad? Her York Street neighbours had that song, *Are you sad little bee? Are you sad?* What a foggy, whimsical year that was in Newfoundland. The kids were babies, Gilles was in Alaska. Her friendship with Erin was the most nurturing thing. There had been a reckless sort of abandon between them. Erin's generosity was bottomless. She kept a bag of stuff from the dollar store in a cupboard over her dishwasher and they made Wikki Stix glasses and little dragonflies and finger puppets. Erin would pick up her guitar and sing about monsters or milk moustaches. She was everything Linda could have wished for in a friend. Linda was sick with sadness when it came time to pack up and leave. She didn't want to meet new people. She didn't want to invest in new friendships. After a few months in Winnipeg, Carrie and Marty came along, and although it wasn't the same kind of kindred, it was cozy and fun in that under-ground wine bar. She didn't sink in though. Why set yourself up for future sorrow? Which reminds her, she has to confirm Carrie and Marty's new mailing address for Christmas cards. They were posted last summer. Marty had shared a picture of their Yucca tree on Instagram, wilted after four days inside a moving truck.

"Shit!" Gilles yells, leaning into the steering wheel as a glossy animal bounces off the windshield. They swerve to the right. The front of the car lightens when the tires hit loose gravel. Gilles wrestles with the wheel as the car slides.

It isn't an animal but a black garbage bag, and it doesn't come apart right away, but volleys off the windshield and flies over the top of their car, catching on the railing of the roof rack, where it tears open. Gilles gets the car back on the road as garbage spews past the back seat windows and the rear windshield. Cans, cardboard, paper coffee cups, a flourish of nondescript detritus in their wake, as if the car is blasting out of a dumpster. A flier sticks to Stephen's window, flapping: Reliable Heating and Cooling Ltd., Almonte.

Gilles's posture is upright, rigid, an exaggerated straight-ness, his two hands cemented on the wheel as they decelerate. A crackling hiss as the empty bag, still hanging on to the roof rack, flaps in the wind like a mainsail.

"Jesus!" he says. "Fuck me."

"Whoa." Linda touches his arm as she hands him her water bottle. "Language, love," she hushes.

Gilles glares at her. The iPad is open on her lap.

"I thought it was a bear," Stephen says from the back seat.

Linda turns to the kids. "Everyone okay?"

"ANOTHER ONE!" Sophia points and shouts, her eyes bulging.

A second bag of garbage flies out of the pickup truck that is well ahead of them now. The bag rolls and bounces in the wind, then flies off the road. Bumbling into the trees, it splits and scatters pieces of Styrofoam in a climactic smithereen pomp, tiny white specks swirling in the wind and dispersing like ricochets.

Gilles slows the car again. Breathes deeply.

"Want me to drive?"

"No. I just need a minute."

"You sure?"

"Yes."

Linda checks her leaderboard. The time has elapsed. She made it! Barely. Duo the owl is lying down, exhausted, zzz's floating. *Congratulations Linda, you finished in ninth place in the Diamond league. Complete a lesson to join a new leaderboard.*

Excited to see what the next league will be, she starts a new lesson in the section on routine.

Write this in English.
Quiero ir al cine con mis amigos.
I want to go to the movies with my friends.
BING DONG Nicely done!

She finishes the lesson. On her new leaderboard there's Mimi6, DarkeK, Anne Cobs, Livio, Jean42Caro, FMonahan. HoboLu has a photo of lily pads for their profile picture. But wait! It's still the diamond league.

Linda refreshes her page. Diamond league.

"I didn't advance," she says in a panic. "I'm still in the diamond league."

"Something wrong with the app? Can you report it?" Gilles says, his face still pale.

Linda Googles — *Duolingo after diamond league* — *after reaching diamond league: duolingo* — *Reddit* — *Gamifying the gamification of the language game* — *no more promotion zone after diamond league* — *ladder of leagues reaches the diamond league in Duolingo* —

"The diamond league is the highest level," she says, deflated. "No more promotion after the diamond league. Only demotion."

Gilles pats her leg. "Look at you! Duolingo Diamond Leaguer!"

"It's disappointing," she says as she tucks the iPad into the glove compartment.

"We'll get through this." He smiles at her.

"Don't mock me. I like my Duolingo world, seeing progress, making gains."

"Why don't you Google some schools in Colorado Springs?"

She stares out the window, ignoring him.

"I thought you were happy about Colorado."

"I am . . . but I don't know. Another move. Such a brain drain."

"What's going on, love? And anyway, why are you shopping for coffins . . ."

"I wasn't shopping for coffins, Gilles, it just gave me pause," she says. "I saw coffins at Costco, and it gave me pause." Gilles reaches for her hand now, rubs his thumb over her knuckles. "I just . . . the idea of another move, packing up our life again . . ." she says.

They continue in silence as they drive through the outskirts of some remote northern Ontario town. Outside a large truck and trailer dealership, a line of bright yellow dump trucks, about twenty of them, are parked with their dump boxes raised. Linda imagines that the cabs are heads with their bare necks exposed. "Also, I'm going to stop watering my plants. I'm just going to let them die in peace."

"Okay, not peaceful."

"Well, I don't want to shove them into a boiling hot moving truck where they'll bake for seven days in the dark."

"Give them to someone."

Linda's eyes linger on the passing trees. They are priggish in the violent wind. Slight and jerky movements, they could be hard plastic. "Who, though?" she asks, still staring out the window. "Who would I give my plants to?"

"Sonny the Rooster!" Sophia cries from the back seat. "It's Sonny! What's that stuff all around him?"

"He's boarded up," Stephen says.

Sonny is a construction zone. Slats of board cordon off the space around the giant rooster, and a black garbage bag is wrapped around its wattle, which has been damaged. The pale green Styrofoam interior is visible, and morsels of Styrofoam are scattered among the fruit and nuts of the horn of plenty below the rooster's clawed feet.

"Vandals?" Linda says, lowering her window as they approach Sonny. The wind is bitterly cold on her face, causing her eyes to water.

"What are vandals?" Sophia asks.

"It might have been the storm," Gilles says. "There was a major storm in this region on Wednesday." He puts the car in park and slumps back in his seat. "What do you want to do?"

"I want us to stand in front of Sonny and smile."

"Great," Gilles says. "And don't worry about the mess, I can blur the background."

The camera is set up. Gilles uses bricks and pieces of wood that are scattered near the base of the rooster to secure his tripod in the wind. Standing in front of Sonny, the four of them bend their knees a little as they lean into the wind, smiling. Their eyes water, their hair is blown in the same sideways direction, and if one didn't look too closely, if, during the hectic holiday season, one cast only a passing glance, the natural conclusion would be that this family is brimming with wishes for a joyous holiday season and a prosperous New Year.

GWEN THE CASTLE

"Can you take my picture?" A man holds out his phone to the woman. His other hand is in the pocket of an oversized black peacoat under which he wears a bulky hoody. The man's eyes are sunken, cement-grey, and so deeply set that shadows fill the crescent hollows below and above them. On first glance, she is reminded of a raccoon. In those first moments, something feral. Actually, no, the woman thinks, I'd rather enjoy the scenery. She smiles and takes his phone.

The woman's name is Gwen.

Gwen has been leaning against the railing of a ferry that will take her to an artist's residency on Toronto Island for the long weekend. She fumbles with her tote, hesitates for a moment to situate a compelling background, a leading line, a depth of field.

"It doesn't matter," the man says. "The background doesn't matter." His expression is ridiculing and impatient, and Gwen gnaws the inside of her cheek. She would like to say, *Would*

you like to take it yourself, asshole? She smiles though, takes three pictures, tapping his face on the screen to draw light upon it, shifting him into the bottom left third of the frame, adjusting the angle so that the background is the lake and the horizon instead of the red plastic bin labelled *Children's Life Jackets,* that is covered in a layer of dust in which someone has traced a large dick.

She hands the phone back to him. "Thanks," he says, slipping it into his pocket without looking at the pictures she has taken. "I'm Kevin."

"Myra," she lies.

"You're staying at the Airbnb? On the island?" His leg brushes against her luggage as he leans over the railing next to her. "I like your blue hair by the way. Very aquamarine."

She had let her ten-year-old daughter dye a blue streak in her brown hair last week. "Visiting a friend, actually," she lies again, staring out at the water and the cluster of boxy, colourful houses on the coast.

"I like to come to the island every so often to get away from the lunacy." He nods toward Toronto's harbourfront, distant now, the CN Tower exalting from the city-line like a spear. His eyes shift to the tripod that's strapped to her back. "Let me guess, photographer? I just had a book published last year and I worked with Kyle Rensfeld. Incredible eye. It's on Amazon, my book. *A Toronto Guide to Self-Representation in Court.* Non-fiction. Very niche."

"Kill me now," she does not say. "I'm not a photographer, I just like taking pictures."

Three gulls bob in the water near the docks. A fourth planes down to join the others as the ferry approaches. Inside the marina, a slushy patchwork of ice shifts and rocks slowly with the motion of the water. Gwen stares at the ice and thinks of leopard-print patterns. Her daughter, Jessie, is obsessed with animal prints, and just last week, schooled her on the differences between leopard print and tiger, giraffe, cougar, and zebra print. She urged Gwen to pay close attention to the patterns and the space between the variety of polygonal shapes. They are not just spots, she had said.

Gwen walks off the ferry in search of her host, Leonard, whose welcome email had instructed her to look for the Artscape Van, and there it is. Rainbow block letters hand-painted on the sliding door of a maroon minivan: ARTSCAPE GIBRALTAR POINT.

"Gwen? Hi. Leonard. Welcome!" Leonard takes her luggage. "OMG, what's in here, lead?" He lifts with his legs and throws her bag into the back of the van.

"Books, a shrimp ring, a dozen eggs," she says.

"Shit! Eggs?"

"Kidding." She holds up her tote. "Eggs are in here."

"Very funny," he says. "Glad you arrived safe, and I like your blue hair. Peacocky."

"Thanks. So, people seriously live over here year-round without a grocery store?"

"No biggy. Islanders go back and forth on the ferry. It's a quick and easy jaunt, as you have just experienced." They drive away from the docks, and Gwen sees the Kevin guy from the ferry standing on the side of the road, giving her two thumbs up. Raccoon Man.

As they drive, Leonard's militant delivery of island lore and history have a loosening effect on Gwen. She warms to him, and before long, a stubborn anxiety drifts from her. On the train from Ottawa to Toronto, she wrestled with her choice to leave her daughter this weekend. Jessie started her period last night. She was excited to be the first girl in her class to start. Peter encouraged Gwen to keep her plans. There will never be a good time, Gwen, he had said. You've been planning this for months. You've mailed your canvasses. Go. We'll be fine.

Now, as she stares out the window of the van, she is cradled by the bleakness of the place. Leonard points to a short bridge that connects to another small island and an amusement park. Closed for the season are pizza and ice cream kiosks, a roller coaster, a cedar hedge maze. It's a neat vibe to walk around in there, he tells her. The city demolished all the houses on this side of the island in the fifties to build a public park. No cars allowed except for a few service vehicles. Serenity now.

On the north side of the road, willow trees scrape against the blue sky. Dramatic spikes of ice nest at the base of tree trunks, and icicles hang from branches. Beyond the trees, tall yellow grass sways in the wind and sand ripples toward Lake Ontario, which looks from the road to be as vast as the sea.

The Artscape at Gibraltar Point artist residence is an old school that was saved from the fifties' demolition spree. A squat one-story building with sage-coloured vinyl siding and ancient, grime-covered windows; its wild grounds chitter with squirrels and birds. Inside, Gwen flashes to some early and unusual childhood memory of her nursery school. It's the smell: a mulled concoction of acrylic paint, mildew, and concrete. Or it might be the way the sun filters through the jungle of plants bathing by the windows, or the dusty radiators, their bellies painted creamy yellow. She lugs her things into the kitchen/lounge area, where other artists have gathered for Leonard's mandatory welcome brief.

"Before I forget, sign up here for kitchen clean-up duty. Thank you kindly," he says. He introduces everyone. Caitlyn, a painter of murals, and her boyfriend, Robbie, a digital musician. Jaclyn, a writer who is working on her collection of poetry, titled *Herbal Remedies for the End of the World*. Garth, also a writer. Sarah, a Persian dancer who is preparing a dance workshop. "We have our long-term resident artists as well. You'll see them come and go and meander. Jamie is a puppeteer, Mitchell's a painter. Lynette and Monica are working on a large-scale installation for Nathanial Square. Lots going on. I'm sure everyone will get along famously. This common area is where we gather and share, or not share. My office is right off the kitchen if you need me during the day."

Leonard leads the group through dim corridors. Mounted on the walls are quilts and paintings and sculptures, including a wood carving of *The Giraffodill*: a giraffe's body with a one-eyed daffodil for a head. Its eye peers at Gwen as if examining her pores, and she is giddy — that delightful sensation that overwhelms her when she is surrounded by creatives. A showcase encloses a collection of taxidermy waterbirds set against a shoreline with leaves, rocks, and shrubs. The birds' glass eyes, dusty and incredulous. "Please do enjoy the original decor of these teensy drinking fountains. We even have an original eyewash station circa 1964." Inside the taxidermy bird case, the webbed foot of a wood duck has been bent and pinned to a papier mâché rock. "The tap water is safe for drinking," Leonard continues. "Matter of fact, the water purification plant is across the street. L'eau de source!" he boasts. "Here are your keys, lefty lockey, righty unlockey. Keep them on you. Occasionally, we get weirdos who wander over to this side of the island. Not so much in the winter, but we ask that you keep your doors locked."

In the evening, Gwen bundles up for a walk. Across the street from the school, a cement lighthouse looms majestic with its door and rooftop painted a gaudy red. A plaque documents the unconfirmed story of the first lighthouse keeper who disappeared mysteriously, a human skeleton found nearby, legend that the building is haunted. Gwen welcomes the spook of it. The Toronto skyline glistens rosy gold and she can hear faint sirens and horns. The lunacy, he had said. Raccoon Man from the ferry with his niche non-fiction.

She continues her walk to the beach. Rust and charcoal-coloured sediment threads through pale sand, making tiers, and the sun dips below the horizon. Gwen inhales deeply, listening to the sound of her breath and the lake. That's when she sees it. Something hanging. A white bodily figure hanging from a tree.

She wavers, catches her breath, stares in awe.

The figure is a blouse.

A blouse. She exhales. A sleeveless blouse on a clothes hanger. Up close, she discovers items glued to the shoulders. A tiny plastic wolf on the left, a seashell on the right, a patch of red wool woven into the bottom hem of the sheer white fabric. Mood. She texts Emilie, *This place is full of eerie little marvels. I am so happy. Thank you for setting this up for me.*

Gwen met Emilie Lewis at Meadowlands Elementary school three years ago. They were volunteering together, decorating the gym for a princess and pirate dance. Gwen had painted a castle mural in an elaborate gothic collegiate style — buttresses and parapets, brilliant stained-glass windows —

and it caught Emilie's attention. Emilie was a well-known artist in the city and had a gallery downtown.

"So, you're Gwen, the castle," she said the first time they met. "You need to come by my studio." She gave her books to read, movies to watch, took her to museums and art shows. They studied Klee, Klimt, Emily Carr, Shary Boyle, Agnes Martin, Riopelle, Pollock. Gwen's world cracked open.

Back in her Artscape studio, a wall of windows overlooks the backyard. It's dark outside, but she can distinguish the grassy area, snow-covered and surrounded by trees. The beach is just beyond those trees. She unpacks her canvases and her paint and supplies, lines them up against the wall, unrolls butcher paper across the floor until it spans the entire length of the studio. She fills her cups with paint — bronze, beige, burnt amber, and black — and one at a time, pours the paint across the length of the butcher paper. With a squidgy, she pulls the paint, creating ripples in which the bronze dominates. She dips a comb in silicone, dabs the wet paint, and cells of beige and amber emerge, ballooning into each other. Mineral tones and interlocking cells extend the length of the studio. The bronze paint, in patches now, appears almost like scattered scales. With a fine tipped brush, she paints a bright red knit square the size of her palm in the corner of the butcher paper and slowly pours white paint around the red. The paint drools like something molten. The blouse, the beach, the blood. She falls into bed at three a.m., exhausted from exhilaration.

....

The following day, Gwen spends a few hours in her studio before breakfast. She has been working with different techniques and is thrilled by her creations. She works with shades of green and blue, aiming for the green-blue gradient of copper that collects at the base of the icicles on the beach. With a heat gun and her own breath she moves the paint on the paper to creates the stiff glisten of frost — a shocked, rigid opaque. Her studio gleams with winter light from its wall of windows.

I feel like I'm unspooling, she texts Emilie. *I don't even know what time of day it is.*

Unspool away! Emilie responds. *Glad to hear it's going well. Now hide that phone. Immerse yourself. Avoid any and all interruptions.*

Gwen breaks for tea, works again, breaks for lunch, then works until her back and neck ache. In the evening, she bundles up for another sunset walk.

It is windier this evening, and the sleeveless blouse is not hanging, but soaring parallel to the ground. There are no birds. There is no one. It *is* serenity now, she thinks as she follows a wooden boardwalk that connects the beach back to the road. The sun has set, but there is ambient light from the moon and the water treatment plant. When she reaches the road, she startles at the appearance of a tall man wearing a black peacoat over a bulky hoody.

"Myra?" he says as cold air clouds around his face. She can see his sunken grey eyes, their raccoon shadows, and she stiffens. There is no one around. She locks in place and her mind floods with horrifics. Limbs, yawning mouths, throats, hands, bare thighs, bruised forearms, and the empty beach, the see-through blouse, the red patch, the water treatment plant. There are no birds, just grains of sand and rippling lines. A see-through sleeveless blouse soaring in icy air.

He backs away from her. Shrugs his hands out of his pockets and holds them up like a shield, as if she is pointing a water hose at him. He must sense her fright. He looks meek now, embarrassed, and Gwen, lightheaded from holding her breath, recognizes this particular expression of unsteadiness. The flex of cheek muscles when both hope and agony are present on the face; the instant when something possible morphs into something denied. Her daughter's face does this when Gwen objects to something she's asked for. To be on the receiving end of this particular face is to participate in the disappointment.

"You came again, to the islands," she says. "It's such a long walk."

"It's just an hour's walk from the docks. Maybe a little more than an hour. I was hoping to bump into you. I was thinking maybe we could hang out?"

"Oh," Gwen says. "No. No, I'm working this week."

His expression darkens. "Working?" He cocks his head. "You said you were visiting a friend."

"I'm . . ."

"Well," he interrupts, "can I at least show you the beach?"

"No, I think I'll head back." She walks in the direction of the residency.

"I'll walk with you?"

"I'm good."

"Wait," he says. "Are you married or something?"

"Yes," she says, turning her head slightly as she walks away from him. "And I have a daughter."

"Oh. That explains the reticence."

Her eyes fix on her feet as she walks. Listening for him behind her, she picks up her pace, speed walks, then breaks into a run as she enters the schoolyard. Removing her mittens, she fumbles her key into the lock. Inside, the hallway is dark except for the kitchen's glow. The others are making dinner. A yeasty smell of curry and fish, electronic music, a lyric-less whirling, and her heart pounds. She can feel its pressure in her chest, the swell and sink of it, and she bends to the floor, hands first, then knees. She sits on the floor with her back against the wall and loosens her scarf which is soaked from her breath and sweat. On the ceiling, water stains look like jellyfish creeping between two tiles. Nausea sweeps over her.

"Gwen?" Leonard zips his coat to his chin as he approaches. "What's going on?"

"I'm trying to think . . . I'm trying to think if I . . . on the ferry, if I . . ."

He helps her up and leads her into his office where she tells him what's happened. "I'm on my way home now," he says. "I'll speak to the guys at the docks. They'll keep an eye out." He scribbles notes as he speaks to her. "We can't have weirdos creeping around this place. I'm sorry this happened to you, Gwen."

Later, in her studio, Gwen is unable to relax or focus. While mixing her paint, she is startled by her own reflection in the windows. If only there were curtains or blinds. She positions one of her blank canvases on the table and prepares her paint, but her gaze keeps darting to the windows. The last ferry leaves the island at eleven p.m. Surely, he isn't still wandering around out there, it's too cold. She prepares cups of red, gold, black, and white paint, adding a drop of silicone to each cup, then combining them. She places the canvas on top of the cup and flips it, lifting the cup slowly as the paint flows and takes shape. Colours seep into a form that she torches for a few seconds to prevent blending. The form stretches, yawns gold and red and black, and she is pleased with the dynamic contrasts as she tilts the canvas in a continuous motion. She freezes then. A figure in the window. She strains her eyes at the sudden movement outside and her heart is pounding. She stares and stares, but all she can see is her own reflection, standing with the canvas in her hands as if making an offering. Her trembling causes the paint to shiver and blend.

In the kitchen, Gwen makes a cup of chamomile tea before returning to her studio and her canvas, where the red paint has completely blended with white and paled to a pasty mauve. The original colours have lost their value. She can't stop glancing at the windows. She imagines him standing in the backyard with his hands in his pockets.

That night, Gwen awakens to a violent banging on her window. On her hands and knees, cloaked in her comforter, she creeps across her bed. She stands near the cold wall next to the window, her nose brushing against the edge of the curtain. His face is on the other side of this thin pane of glass, his fist banging, his sunken eyes searching inside. The wind drones and the pane shifts, knocking back and forth.

It is the wind. It is the wind that is banging.

Gwen's entire body is heavy with dread as she peeks from behind the curtain. Gusts of snow drift across the vacant yard to the road. Her bladder is full, but the bathroom is across the hall, and she is too spooked to leave her room. At 3:24 a.m., it is so quiet that when she squats over her garbage tin, the sound of urine hitting the rusty bottom echoes and swirls all around her, and she imagines that she is inside an amber marble.

....

The following day in her studio, Gwen is listless and unproductive. An emerging ache in her pelvis reminds her that her period is coming, and she is exhausted from a night of disrupted sleep. The beachscape she had delighted in yesterday looks childish and laboured today. She doesn't know where to start, so she organizes and reorganizes her materials until their tidiness feels sterile and oppressive.

Around noon in the kitchen, Robbie is frying salmon, and Caitlyn is tossing a salad.

"How's it going?" Caitlyn asks.

"Today isn't a good day." Gwen opens the fridge and removes her shrimp ring. She presses her fingers into her lower back. "How's your mural?"

"Not bad. You should drop by to see it before you leave tomorrow," she says. "We're heading to the amusement park after lunch. Come with us! Leonard told us about the creepy dude from the ferry."

Gwen peels plastic from the sauce that's nested in the centre of her shrimp ring. "Thanks, yeah. I'm totally spooked." She dips a shrimp. "I Googled him. His book." Gwen brings up his face on her phone.

"He looks bored," Caitlyn says. Robbie leans in behind her.

"Lonely fucker," he says.

"A lawyer, according to his author bio," Gwen says. "His name is listed at TLR Law. I know where he works, where he lives."

"Seriously?" Caitlyn mumbles through a mouthful of lettuce.

"The only Kevin McCauley on Canada 411 lives at 279 Palmerston Avenue. Took me less than thirty seconds."

"Okay, now who's creepy?" says Caitlyn. Gwen shrugs, massaging her lower back. "You look like you're in pain. There are yoga mats in the hall closet."

"I just started my period."

"That sucks. There might be some tampons in the first-aid kit."

"I've got my Diva Cup."

"They are seriously the best."

. . . .

Outside, it is a beautiful winter day. No clouds, just blue, and the beach can be heard from the road as Gwen, Caitlyn, and Robbie walk to the amusement park.

"I'm gonna check out this maze," Gwen says as she branches off from the pair and pulls her camera out of its case. Caitlyn and Robbie walk over the bridge toward the kiosks and the roller coaster. "I'll catch up."

The William Meany Maze is made of tall cedar hedges that are now peppered with snow and ice. Gwen enters and winds through the labyrinthine passages, her footsteps crunching. She takes a picture around a corner, shifting the angle to slant the sides of the hedge with a slice of sky. She zooms in on an ice-fossilized footprint, then captures the inside of the maze, a moat of evergreen. She looks up from her lens when she hears another set of footsteps. They wind closer and farther away from her, pausing, turning. At one point, it seems they are just on the other side of the hedge. The steps stop for a moment before starting again. Gwen freezes. The footsteps continue, and then around the corner, an elderly woman in a puffy beige parka appears. Bundled in a scarf, the woman doesn't notice Gwen. She is looking at her feet, and when she finally sees Gwen, she startles, paws at her chest with her wool mittens and drops her water bottle.

"Jesus!" she yells. "You startled me!"

Gwen picks up the bottle. "I'm so sorry."

"Why were you just standing there like that? God!" the woman says, exasperated. "You scared me." She exhales a hiss, and scowls at Gwen as she walks past her, snatching the bottle. Gwen fastens her camera back into its case and walks in the opposite direction, out of the maze. She can see Caitlyn and Robbie on the other side of the bridge taking a selfie in front of a bright green kiosk, and in her peripheral, the elderly woman cuts across the grass to the road.

"Hi, Myra. Or is it Gwen?"

Raccoon Man. He is leaning on the outside of the maze with his arms crossed.

"Why are you here?"

"I want you to listen to me," he says, walking toward her. "I felt a strong connection to you on the ferry. I felt it. It was real." His voice is warm and unhurried. "Why did you tell me your name was Myra? Is that your middle name? Is Myra your middle name, Gwen?"

She retreats. Small backward steps.

"And today, I was specifically drawn to this place, and here you are." She turns then, to walk away from him. "Myra? Don't you think it's something? Can't we just talk? Why are you being so cold? Gwen? Please? I just want to talk. For fucksake, I just want to talk to you."

Gwen runs across the bridge to where Caitlyn and Robbie are taking another selfie in front of a closed-for-the-season, bright yellow ice cream shop that has the words *I Scream, You Scream* handwritten above the concession window. "Caitlyn," she yells, breathless, "guys, it's him — the guy . . . from the ferry. It's fucking *him!* Again. I'm going to lose my mind."

Back at the residency, Leonard is standing on a ladder watering the plants in the kitchen.

"Hey, Leonard! Gwen introduced us to her stalker." Robbie unwinds his scarf as he puts the kettle on the stove.

"Yes, Gwen, we need to talk." Leonard climbs down from the ladder. "He came here looking for you. I heard a banging on the front door, and when I went to answer it, it was this guy I didn't recognize as one of my artists. He asked for Myra. I told him we didn't have a Myra here at Artscape Gibraltar Point. Then he said she has this blue-green streak of hair, and without thinking, I said, 'You must mean Gwen.'"

"You told him my name, Leonard?"

"I'm sorry. Really, I am. I didn't realize . . ." Leonard hands her a yellow manilla envelope. "He gave me this package for you."

She tears open the envelope. It's his book: *A Toronto Guide to Self-Representation in Court.* As she flips through the pages, a letter drops to the floor.

"Jeez. It is unfortunate though," Leonard continues, "because we can't do anything unless there is an act of aggression. We can't actually keep him off the island. I asked."

Gwen spends most of the evening on a ladder in her studio, covering the windows with butcher paper. She prepares a canvas but can't decide on the colour palette. She selects a number of blues, and the bronze she'd been working with, but decides to try a dark violet instead, with gold cells. Or maybe the red with gold cells. Her stomach cramps are severe, and her lower back aches as she stares at the white canvasses. Agony. Her last night in the studio. She's tired and miserable and has failed to produce anything exciting. Now she is spiralling, unable to decide on form, colour, approach. Frustrated, she leaves her studio and walks down the dark hallway to the east wing.

Music is playing, electronic and upbeat, and Caitlyn is in her bare feet, painting a honeycomb mural on canvas she's stretched across the walls. She has painted the entire studio in honeycomb, each cell a different colour. No pattern is clear, but the yellow and coral shades dominate, and instead of bees, tiny colourful zebras surround the honeycomb structure.

"Amazing," Gwen says. "You've done this since Friday?"

"I have! I was able to get into a really good groove," she says. "How about you?"

"Not so much."

"I'm sorry."

"I love the rainbow zebras," Gwen says as she looks closely at them. Jessie would be impressed. "You up for a quick walk on the beach? There's a beautiful moon."

"That sounds awesome," Caitlyn says.

On the beach, they walk past the pier to a rusty swing set. The lake is calm and glinting beneath the moon. Gwen wonders if he is lurking somewhere nearby. Might he appear and drain the joy from this moment? I refuse to ignore this serendipity, his letter had said.

What if it was Jessie, she thinks. What if her daughter was spooked by a guy like that? Gwen feels a sort of adrenaline. She's furious. Furious with his leisure to hijack her weekend.

"He's a parasite," she says to Caitlyn as they soar back and forth on the creaking swings. "I'm not afraid of him. I'm pissed actually. I'm really pissed off."

"But you have to be careful, Gwen. People like that, you just don't know, right? So unpredictable. You don't know what they're capable of."

From the swings, Gwen sees the waterbirds dive. They remain below the water for what seems like a long time before resurfacing.

Back in her studio, Gwen lays the canvasses on the floor. She splatters them with deep violet paint. She doesn't clean her brush before dipping it into the bronze. SPLAT. Turquoise

SPLAT. Vicious, she throws rough lines of paint at the canvas and lets her brush dribble snail-like forms at random. She squirts an almost-empty bottle of bright pink paint, creating tiny dots and droplets, blowing the existing lines to create wrinkles and shivers. Her body warms as she jumps around the canvasses, spraying and splattering and slapping the paint into a molten mess. It dries into what looks like chunky bubble gum stretched and sprawled. The colours have blended, and their syrupy appearance is frantic and disgusting, Gwen thinks. Like something vomited. Something ruined and pathetic. She packs up the canvasses. At home, she'll scrape and sand and start over. What a waste.

. . . .

The following morning, Gwen gazes out the window of the van during the ride back to the docks.

"I hope you had a productive few days," Leonard says. Gwen rolls her eyes. "Hey, isn't that your guy?"

Gwen sits up in her seat. "You've got to be kidding me." Raccoon Man is walking toward the residency. His hands in his pockets.

"He is one determined dude," Leonard says. "I'm sorry, again. It's good you were still able to get some work done."

Gwen stares at the shoreline as they drive past. It's not good. It is not good the way she lets ruin seep into her life. Why does she have to be this porous, floating entity, tousled by whatever weather comes her way? What is it about her that would attract someone like Kevin? Did he sense something inside of her that was infinitely accommodating? Was it the blue streak in her hair?

Every so often there's a lifeguard's chair with lifesaving equipment leaning against it. A chrome lifesaving hook, a red and white lifesaving ring. The equipment seems theatrical among the icicles. She thinks of the blouse hanging from the tree and wonders how long before it is tossed into the lake. Maybe it will remain on the tree, its fibres gradually deteriorating in the elements. The blouse threadbare with the tiny wolf and shell hanging onto the shoulder seams with concrete cement, or some other toxic adhesive.

"What time is your train?"

"Not until this evening. I'm going to drop my bag at Union Station and browse. Probably Koreatown for lunch."

Gwen takes the subway to Christie Station and walks down Bloor until she arrives at Palmerston Avenue. She skips up the front steps of #279 and rings the doorbell. No answer. She rings again. Nothing. She tries the front door. Locked. Searches beneath the welcome mat for a key. Nothing. Mailbox. Empty. She considers breaking his window and slinking through, but no. She examines the windows over the deck, pushes up to see if they might slide open. No luck. She walks around the side of the house, checking basement windows, which are all locked. Finally, she checks the back door, which opens to the heavy, powdery scent of fabric softener. Of course he keeps his door open, she thinks. She lets herself in.

His kitchen is modern. A stainless-steel range hood suspends from the ceiling over a gleaming white granite island. A leather armchair sits in the corner by the window with a pile of books and files and magazines arranged neatly on the floor next to it. *Birds of Ontario*, *Men's Health*, and a magazine with a cover picture of a bronze Lady Justice, blindfolded, holding a scale above her head, the title caption "CBA/ABC National: Protecting Judicial Independence in the Age of Populism." The entire place is neat and orderly like a show home. When the dryer buzzes and shuts off, she hears a shuffling, squeaking sound in the next room. On the dining table, a cage is home to three guinea pigs. One is sleeping and the other two are moving about, poking their noses through the rungs of the cage as if they can smell her, are excited by her presence.

Gwen considers smashing things. Stealing something, tearing pages out of magazines, turning on faucets, turning off heat. Something in addition to what she has planned. There is a set of three paintings on the wall in the dining room: French storefronts, euro-style, generic, burgundy awnings and cobblestone streets. Boulanger, Patissier, Fromagerie. She tilts each painting so that they hang askew. Mood.

In the bathroom, on the toilet, she removes her Diva Cup. It is three quarters full of blood.

She wipes herself, fixes a pad to her panties, fastens her jeans, and then, as if anointing, dips her finger into the blood and flicks it across the bathroom mirror and faucet. Small pinpoint drops. She walks down the hallway flicking. In his bedroom, she flicks larger drops now, blood on his pillow, his mirror, his bedside lamp. She pours drops of blood on her hand, covers her palm with it, and leaves a handprint on the armrest of a lime green chair. In his closet, she handprints his breast pockets. She walks through his house splattering every window, every light fixture, flicking blood onto the leaves of the single houseplant, a large, leggy umbrella tree. The droplets sit on the leaves like beady insects. On the white granite island in the kitchen, she pours the remaining contents of the Diva Cup and lets it pool ruby. With her finger, she wisps lines outward, like quills, or spikes, or a blossom.

A cup of tea, she thinks, and she boils the kettle. Sitting at the kitchen island, sipping on her tea, Gwen glances around, allowing her gaze to settle on the tiny, beautiful beads of red that are everywhere. Pure rich red. Before leaving his house, she opens the guinea pig cage. One wobbles over to her, and she lifts it up, nestles it under her chin, then sets it down on the floor, leaving the cage door swinging open like a wing.

PORTRAIT OF A MOTHER

In the evenings, my mother often walked with her friend Sheila. Bundled up with neck warmers and earmuffs, they marched along the streets of Happy Valley, Labrador, swinging their arms, breaking a sweat, attempting to shed a few pounds. My sisters and I mocked their speed-walking gait and their gossiping, but some nights I joined her. Mother liked to look into people's houses to see how they positioned their furniture, their artwork. She was most interested in dining rooms and their tables. "The table's the hub," she always said. "It's where the magic happens."

Mother had gorgeous breasts. Unsupported, they surrendered, but elevated with taut material, they were exquisite. They punctuated her shape. Ever focussed on her posture, she considered it the canvas on which her glorious bosom was presented. Back straight, shoulders rooted. A family portrait of my mother and her seven younger siblings hangs in our grandparents' dining room. Of her straight-backed posture Aunt Roslyn says, "Would you look at Mary, she's planted."

Our childhood dining room was the hub of our household. Two windows flanked an oval oak table surrounded by six chairs. One of the windows opened to a clothesline and oftentimes, in the midst of a Labrador winter, my mother would lean her whole self outside, tow the screeching line, and fill a laundry basket with frozen stiff clothing that was tinselled with icicles. Gradually the clothing thawed, but the scent of frost sustained. A matching oak hutch stood in the corner of the dining room. On Sundays, we'd set the table with Mother's 'fancy' dishes, an ivory set trimmed with coral, brown, and green paisley that she and my father had collected over many months of filling up the Dodge van at Irving's gas station. One full tank scored a plate, a teacup or a salt and pepper shaker. The silver had its own drawer that was lined with red velvet. When we opened the door of the hutch, it breathed on us its crawlspace scent of fresh newspaper and moldy lemon.

During the school year my father sat at the foot of the table, making his way through piles of Canadian History assignments, his cup of tea neat against papers on the Red River Rebellion, the Plains of Abraham, the Canadian Pacific Railway. My two sisters and I also did our homework at that table. Overseeing our efforts was a portrait of a Kenyan woman holding a child. The woman wore a traditional head wrap, and the baby careened slightly, clutching the woman's shawl with his chubby hands, his hair a mess of short tight curls. Both woman and child stared dispassionately at their observer, their vignettes basking in sunlight. Mother had received the portrait as a gift from Margaret, who visited Kenya in 1976. Margaret had observed the pair while the artist created their likeness. She admired the young mother, who remained tranquil amid the chaotic marketplace and thought it befitting of my mother, who, according to Margaret, kept things together in the midst of frenzy. Margaret, a fellow teacher, remained single all her life and passed her summers exploring the globe. Mother used words like *worldly*, *tasteful*, and *sophisticated* to describe her, and the portrait added an element of repute to our otherwise modest dining room. The solemn mother and child attended our everyday rituals, tranquil witnesses to the contents of our days.

....

Elaine lived next door, and I often babysat her two boys, Mark and Christopher. Elaine was short and round with gold specks throughout her grey-blue eyes. Everything about her was generous — her bosom, her bottom, her laughter, her fury.

"Make sure you clean up over at Elaine's, hun," Mother insisted. Elaine's countertops were legendary in their ability to balance stacks of dirty pots and pans. Her house brimmed with the humidity of something just baked — scones or bread or cinnamon rolls. Draped over her dining room table were half-made dresses and gowns and angular shapes of fabric.

Velvet and satin and lace in shades of emerald and sapphire and chartreuse. She was a maker of costumes. Elaine's geometric dress patterns of blue lines and curves, mapped on translucent paper, lay beneath her treasured assortment of buttons and ribbons, zippers and sequins; her seamstress tools sprawled across table and chairs. Beds were unmade, laundry baskets overflowed, but enchanting figure-skating dresses presided on mannequins and racks.

Unlike Elaine, Mother loved order and economy. Her home was an extension of herself, and if it was in disarray, then she too was disquieted. She posted a seasonal meal plan on the fridge door and stocked the freezer with homemade frozen spaghetti, cod au gratin, and cabbage rolls. A similar handwritten list was taped inside her bedroom closet with weekday outfits for a semester. She owned skirts and blouses that were more than ten years old and took meticulous care of them. They were as good as new. She often wished she could be more like Elaine. "God bless her soul. Elaine, the place bottom up, she'll sit in the middle of it, clear a space on her table for coffee, and complain about how lazy the kids are."

....

My sisters and I often accompanied my mother when she visited her elderly friend, Molly. Molly drank whiskey, chain-smoked, and watched *Days of Our Lives,* which she referred to as 'my show.' She also cursed a lot.

Molly told us about her nasty, good-for-nothing husband who used to beat her brutally. He sent her out for a pack of cigarettes one night and she never went back. She moved to Labrador, lived by herself, and worked at the church. Molly was partly deaf, so she yelled her curse words. In the corner of her small dining room, the washer and dryer were tucked beneath a poster of Pope John Paul ii. Her table was cluttered with ashtrays, statues of St. Francis de Sales (patron saint of the deaf), an aquamarine carnival glass dish chock-full of white mints, and a bottle or three of Jack Daniels. A chandelier hung in the centre of the room, its glass beads stained yellow and cloaked in dust. She lived on the top floor of a two-story house, and the stairs to her apartment were steep. Worried that Molly would slip and fall, my mother helped her with groceries and shopping and visited her every week. When Mother died, Molly said she wished it had been her instead. Molly purchased her own casket and took pictures of her sinewy self lying in it, arms crossed, eyes closed. She was ready for anything and as tough as bark, but when Mother moved to Newfoundland for cancer treatment, Molly wept like a child.

....

Mother's new wig gave her a false glamour that was jarring and sad. Her eyes stared out from underneath it, doleful and unsteady. There was an excitable sort of angst in her expression that was also new. The first time she showed me her scars, she said, "They're not that bad. The surgeon did an excellent job." She spoke of the clinic where she met other women who requested reconstructive surgery, because they felt like freaks. "They are young women," she said. "I'd feel worse if I'd lost a tooth."

Doreen and Mother had been roommates in college and taught together in Labrador. Stylish and brazen, Doreen pulled green plastic martini glasses from her purse and made strawberry daiquiris on my mother's hospital room table. She added pink straws and blueberries, said cheers, and told a story about when they first started teaching in Labrador. They were at the officer's nightclub on the air force base when my mother noticed a pale blue rug with black birds. Doreen rolled up the rug and threw it out the window. When they left that night, they picked up the rug and made off like bandits.

"Didn't we piss ourselves laughing, driving away with that rug? It was probably from Argentina."

"It was probably from Sears." Mother hunched over her strawberry daiquiri and slurped until it was gone. When Doreen stepped into the hallway, my mother gazed out the window and said she hadn't changed an ounce. I walked Doreen out. As she wept, she said Mother was a gem and told me I was a lucky duck.

....

Conscious of her sour smell, Mother asked me to bathe her every day. Manoeuvring her into the bath was an enormous strain and the most tender touch caused pain. I lifted her frail, bent body from bed to bath. Once in the water, she released into my arms. I cupped her bald head like an egg and allowed the water to rise past her jawline. Her arms drifted to her sides; her bent legs splayed open. With a sponge, I rinsed her cheeks, her neck, her belly, water running across its three wormlike scars. I apologized for the times I'd been selfish. She closed her eyes and mouthed *thank you.*

Eventually Mother stopped bathing. The speaking also ceased, and communication was limited to facial expressions and weak grunts of gratitude, yearning, and despair. Sometimes she placed her hand on my lap or shoulder and stared, head wobbling atop her feeble neck. My father, sisters, and I sat with her amid flowers, cards, and Pachelbel's *Canon in D.* We held hands. She squeezed softly. Her breathing slowed until it stopped. She was forty-eight years old.

The morning she died, I stayed in her room for a few minutes after everyone left. She had become small and gaunt. I lay in the bed beside her, cradled her little head that was warm but still. My pulse vibrated in my chest, and I pressed it against her. Beneath the antiseptic and the septic, I could smell her. Her creamy, musky smell. The room had a large window overlooking the hospital parking lot and the highway. What would it be like out there without her?

After the funeral, my sisters, father, and I returned to our home in Labrador. We agreed that I would keep the portrait of the mother and child from Kenya. When we removed it from the wall, a blue Easter egg dropped to the floor. Like magic. A relic from a long-ago hunt. For years, I kept the portrait in my dining room. When my children were born, I moved the portrait into the nursery, and while nursing my babies, I often stared at the portrait and wondered what Mother would think of my mothering. When my sister's first child was born, I packed up the portrait and shipped it to her home in London, England, Easter egg enclosed.

....

Sometimes I see my mother standing in line at a grocery store. She tilts her head and picks up a *Chatelaine* magazine. On a bus she crosses her legs, stares out the window, twirls an earring. In my neighbourhood she's in her yard, leaning, digging, pruning, making her garden grow. My three children adore her because she bakes on demand. She stores drop molasses cookies in Tupperware containers in the freezer just for them. She watches Disney movies with them all day long and buys them cheap plastic toys even when we ask her not to. She lets them sleep in her bed with her, she scratches their backs. Her cheeks smell of cream and she sings to them . . . *tu ra loo ra loo ra, 'tis an Irish lullaby*. They sink into her bosom like velvet.

I search for Sheila, Elaine, Margaret, Molly, and Doreen in every person I meet, but mostly I search for Mother. I find precious glimpses of her now and then. In the evenings, I bundle up, speed walk, and break a sweat trying to shed a few pounds as I gaze into people's houses, checking the placement of dining room tables and artwork, desperately seeking magic.

A PESSOA GUIDE TO A BIRTHDAY

You find yourself alone in Lisbon on your birthday. In the old world, you are getting old, but do not despair. Place your trust in Lisbon's cherished poet, Fernando Pessoa, and his fragmented *Book of Disquiet*. Keep it close. Let us begin.

We, all who live, have a life that is lived and another life that is thought.

Be sure to greet the morning with gusto. Throw open the ten-foot window shutters. Inhale the humid musk of the blue-flowering jacarandas and stare at the sun in all its optimism. Look out over the great hilled city, its pink, maroon, and yellow rows of connected houses, its ceramic rooftops, its cranes and wrought-iron fences. Wonder, absently, what your beloved mother may have noticed in this city during her travels. Lisbon was her favourite.

Breakfast with your new kindred friend, Renaissance, who requests to be addressed as Ren. Ren is so thin that your grandmother from Newfoundland would have said she could be drawn through the eye of a needle. Ren, whose hair is white and fine, avoids the subject of age. She runs every morning and lifts weights at the machines in the park while roosters march alpha-like at her feet. Admire Ren's gumption to retire from her job in bio-medical research, sell her San Francisco Potrero Hill home, and live here at the Palacio Airbnb, which was once an Austro-Hungarian embassy. Admire also, her plan to travel at whim until she drops off the flat edge of the earth. These are her words. You know very well that the earth is an oblate spheroid whose mass is in constant motion. Ren prefers to travel alone and is loath to waste spirit on such menial things as the coordination of schedules or tourist must-sees and so on. Like Pessoa, she craves time in all its duration; prefers to be by herself unconditionally. Commit to memory Ren's face, expressive with its lines that morph as she says *hideous* when referring to her daughter's recent purchase of a battery-operated pepper shaker that lights up as it dispenses. *Hideous*.

Note how Ren's sudden flare reminds you of your own mother's crankiness. You yearn for a faithful account of your mother in lieu of the platitudes that have transformed her in death to an unrecognizable deity. How her Irish nature could be so mean she'd pick the bruised pear to save a few cents. How she drew breath as she gossiped. Her critical eye. And so, you leech onto every moment that Ren will give. You examine her syllables, the way her skin folds into her collarbone. Surely your mother's skin would have morphed into such rich leafy patterns.

Allow yourself to be enchanted by Ren and her lack of urgency. She seems to have mastered the art of being alone. Did not Pessoa say that freedom is the possibility of isolation? Wonder if you will ever have such liberty. Arrive at the conclusion that this will only be feasible if you come into a sum of money that would allow you to fund your children's college education, that is if they decide to go to college. Concede that it is more likely you will not have such liberty to travel the world solo and maintain your aging cardiovascular system with a morning exercise regime. Unless of course your three children and husband are killed in a gruesome head-on car collision, at which time you will be the sole beneficiary of a sizeable life insurance fund.

In truth, this would be tragic. You would eventually tire of the morning runs beneath the blue-flowering jacarandas, and long for your children and husband and their unconditional love and infinite need. At all cost, resist the urge to dream of winning a large sum of money, as this is a trite and soul-endangering practice. Instead, furnish this day with novel experiences and imaginings. You have time and space on this day. This day, your birthday in Lisbon.

Outside the old embassy front door is a sprawling chessboard of Portuguese mosaic pavement that appears unstable but is solid. The stones shine, having been polished by thousands of soles for thousands of years. Notice the lack of high heels in Lisbon and conform by choosing to wear a low, broad heel. Do not push limits like your eleven-year-old son who is currently at home in Canada eating cinnamon rolls, developing a mouthful of decaying teeth that will cost you a fortune, and prevent you from ever leaving your sleepy hometown again, or at least not before your next milestone birthday, if — unlike your own mother — you make it that far. You'd best enjoy yourself on this day. Why not tap into memories of your mother's joy? When she wasn't contemplating her regret at leaving her teaching career to raise her three children, she experienced joy; there was happiness. Pottering, she called it — free time to potter around her home. How it filled her cup to clean a closet, put sheets on the line, fill a freezer with bread. Could it have been such gestures that provoked ridicule from your adolescent self? When you read about the tiresome pride of Jane Austen's Mrs. Bennet, her lack of tact, her lust for grandeur, her meagre surface-to-substance ratio, a housewife consumed, you thought of your mother. You vowed to lead a larger life. But on your forearm, brown middle-age spots bloom, and your nails are painted maroon. They could be her hands, her arms. Inside your posture, your gait, your rooted shoulders, you feel her bones, you sense her eagerness. You are but her sequel, performing as she did. Does the world find you extraneous? Your disquiet laughable? Does the world ridicule your overwhelm as you did hers? Deep down, does it? A young man shrieks when you step into a section of mosaic pavement that he is repairing with mortar. Shakes his spade in exasperation. Therein lies your answer, perhaps. Or maybe your answer is within the shining mosaic pavement that balloons around you, unstable in places, but mostly solid. The mosaic pavement has been solid for many years and many lives, including that of your mother, and also Pessoa, who shared your sense of disenchantment with the tedium of the modern world. He despaired in the coldness and indifference that surrounded him, yet his search for beauty in small things prevailed: *In this metallic age of barbarians, only a relentless cultivation of our ability to dream can prevent our personality from degenerating into nothing.*

Descend a flight of crooked old stairs. Ignore the fact that you are unsure of your location, and resist the urge to ask Siri, or, worse, consult a map. Either of these actions would diminish the aura of mystery and intrigue that you desire on this day. Recall that Pessoa once declared metaphors more real than the people who walk in the street. You relish a solid metaphor as well as the next person but search not for deeper meaning on this day. You are now in a quiet, well-lit alley and you notice how the row houses loom above you with their open windows and their clotheslines. You can smell the urine and rotting fruit. In truth, it would not be unusual at this time of day to encounter a scene of public urination. Disallow judgement, or worse, repulsion, as this practice is custom in Lisbon proper, and one must accept the grotesque with the beguiling. Carry on, meander, maintaining a spirit of adventure and aplomb. Be not alarmed when you encounter a pigeon that does not scuttle or fly away with your approach. Notice that it simply cocks its head in your direction and continues to hop down the stairs like a four-year-old child. Sink into this new companionship and admire its hopping and its cocking head, its wings tucked prim. Inspect closer and you will notice that its feet are tangled with what looks like dental floss. The pigeon bows its head to peck at its strapped limbs but is powerless against the tangle. It continues to hop, which you now determine is a hobble. It is at this moment that you notice the calico cat perched on a windowsill, eyes fixed on the tethered pigeon, and you cannot prevent yourself from thinking of Pessoa's words on the suffering of others, which passes before us like a nightmare. Press on. Try not to deflate at the thought of the pigeon's impending doom and submit to your unwillingness to risk your own health for its freedom. Recall that you declined health insurance on your plane ticket from Montreal, and if you find yourself debating with yourself, simply imagine this: How on God's green earth will you explain, in Portuguese, your attempt to save a shackled pigeon from a cat? Project further and picture the clinic receptionist, who binds her hair in a floral head-wrap that matches her shawl, on which there is pinned a pewter brooch of an incredulous wide-eyed owl. She thinks you are a fool, meandering uninvited in her country with your sun visor, taking photos of clotheslines and roosters, saving pigeons, which, to her, are equally as irritating as tourists.

Pull yourself together. Meditate on the concept of the textured moment: the texture of emotion that can occur within the space of a moment. Love, anxiety, competition, gratitude, aggression, anger, and confusion. Realize that all these things can occur at the same time. Those moments of intensity that Pessoa tenderly contemplated: *The painful intensity of my sensations, even when they're happy ones; the blissful intensity of my sensations, even when they're sad.* But hurry along now. Do not meditate the day away. It's your birthday, you are in Lisbon, and it is time for lunch, so you'd best stop with your dilly-dallying.

Peruse the restaurants of curiosity that cozy this narrow street until you find one that oozes with promise. Preferably, choose a tiny bistro, *tigelinha* in Portuguese, whose menu is handwritten without English. Inside the tigelinha, choose a table for two and a menu item. Simply point to something, anything at all. Avoid deliberation and trust that today is your day. Four decades ago, the stars aligned for you on this day, and they will align again if you let them. On the day you were born, your mother stared at the Atlantic Ocean from the rugged coast of another continent. Soon you will be presented with an unsolvable riddle as you exceed your mother in age. But this is not a time for brooding on being motherless. Think not of Pessoa's rumination on ships and sailing: *There are ships sailing to many ports, but not a single one goes to where life is not painful.* Snap out of it! Point at your menu choice and smile at your friendly waiter who is older and smilier than you. Have faith. Wait on the wine choice until after your meal arrives, as this selection is something you dare not leave to the stars. What do the stars know of wine pairings? Remind yourself that this is not a day for idle tomfoolery.

Allow fleeting eye contact with the group of six women who are seated at the table directly to your left. The matriarch sets a plastic container in the centre of the table. There are perhaps a few daughters and granddaughters, a cousin. The folds in their faces reveal their kinship. Dark crescents beneath their eyes appear during laughter. Pay close attention to these linked women and their rhythms. You do not understand their words, but their cadence is transparent, and you absorb the crescendos of their conversation. You radiate alongside them. Their postures are relaxed; they make faces. You notice a welling sensation in your throat and sinuses. Deep breathing through the nose is encouraged to stifle this sudden perco-lation. Recall Pessoa's private musings on the feelings that hurt the most: *The absurdity of longing for impossible things; nostalgia for what never was; the desire for what could have been.* Consider your mother's mother (rest her own tethered soul), who would have scoffed at the notion of melancholy. Yet another clever distraction at this time is to make an entry on your calendar for your annual mammogram appointment. This gesture will almost certainly be successful in the quieting of radiant emotions.

A less depleting strategy during this period of heightened emotion is to imagine the birthday feast that is imminent. Glance at your fellow patrons' plates for inspiration, but dis-allow a coveting of their choices, as this will serve to inflate your own expectations, which is not a desirable effect. Upon the arrival of your oval platter of pan-fried sardines with eye-balls intact, neat against a cylinder of risotto, endeavour to contain your excitement before ordering a nine-ounce glass of Vinho Verde, which translates as green wine, but actually means young wine, and is graced with a natural sparkle. Amidst the foreign conversation, food, and drink, savour this moment. Etch into your permanent memory this sensation of an outline of your own essence against this unfamiliar back-drop. Fret not the discombobulation when the smiley waiter arrives to clear the women's table, leaving dessert plates. Breathe deeply when the matriarch stands, opens the plastic container, and inserts candles into six pastéis de nata. Remain calm as the ladies harmonize in Portuguese, the familial and familiar melody of "Happy Birthday."

At this time, be gentle with yourself. You cannot expect to resist the urge to clap your hands and sing along with the other patrons of the tigelinha. After the young woman extinguishes her candles, wish her a happy birthday, and share quietly that it is also your birthday. It is crucial at this point to remain gracious and return to your solo meal; it is her party, after all. When warm tears trickle freely down your cheeks, remind yourself that these are tears of joy provoked by an incident of meek serendipity in an old and aging world. And if Fernando Pessoa were with you, at this table for two, he might mention those relentless half tones of the soul's con-sciousness, which create in us a painful landscape, an eternal sunset of what we are.

ACKNOWLEDGEMENTS

In Deborah Levy's book *The Cost of Living*, she asks, What is a woman for? What should a woman be? I lean on these questions in the stories of this collection. A number of stories are sacred to me, especially Alison Frost's "Mother's Milk," Paola Ferrante's "When Foxes Die Electric," Lorrie Moore's "Community Life," Karen Russell's "Orange World," Souvankham Thammavongsa's "Slingshot," Edna O'Brien's "The Widow," Julie Hayden's "Day-Old Baby Rats," and Alice Munro's "Miles City, Montana." In Francesca Ekwuyasi's *Butter Honey Pig Bread*, her choice to exclude the ugliness of bulimia felt revelatory to me and changed my mind.

Linda Rui Feng, thank you for your friendship, and your beautiful imagination. Dorota Stoddart, your love of fiction and opera has been a source of animation for me, and for my stories. Melissa Remark, writing sister, thank you for writing with me.

Thank you, Keith Maillard, thesis advisor and story shepherd extraordinaire. Thanks also to my professors and friends at UBC for three formative years. A group of early readers have shaped many of these stories: Thank you to Nathan

Mang, Paige Cooper, Evan J, Frances Boyle, Deborah-Anne Tunney, Barbara Sibbald, Debra Martin, Katie Zdybel, Rhonda Douglas, Jaqueline Desforges, and Shelly Kawaja.

Time spent at the Banff Centre had an enormous impact on the stories in this collection. Caroline Adderson, Shyam Selvadurai, Eden Robinson, and Bill Gaston, thank you for your mentorship. Christine Fellows and John K Samson, thank you for your guidance in Winnipeg. I'll never forget it.

Deepest gratitude to the people who let me write in their quiet homes. Linda Rui Feng, Claire Power and Tommy Kelly, Evita Strobele, Nancy Byrne, and Florence Careen Power.

Most of these stories have appeared in literary magazines and anthologies, and the quality of care given to my work by the following editors was remarkable. Iain Higgins at *The Malahat Review*, Pamela Mulloy at *The New Quarterly*, Alyssa McArthur at *Room*, Cameron Maynard at *Carve*, and Marta Balcewicz at *Minola Review*. Thank you, *Riddle Fence, Malahat*, PEN Canada, *The Toronto Star, Prairie Fire*, Bath Short Story Prize, and *The New Quarterly* for seeing something in my stories that was worthy of your fiction awards. Most recently, thank you to Lisa Moore for including my work in *Best Canadian Stories 2024* (Biblioasis).

A far and wide thank you to my military community, especially Angie and Eric Kenny, Mike French, Andrea Greening, Jen DeGroot, Evelyn Stajniak, Erik Doucet, and Nevin Surette for answering my questions about fighter jets, bagpipes, and

RMC in February. Catherine Desmerais, Nicole Drouin, Mariana Davidovitch, Helen Booth, Susan Smith, and all my military spouse friends, thank you for your invisible work and resilience, which are, in fact, not invisible at all.

Thank you to Kelsey Attard, Naomi Lewis, and Colby Stolson at Freehand. What a delight it has been to work with you. Thank you also to Sam Haywood and Devon Halliday at Transatlantic, and Natalie Olsen for the wonderfully weird cover design.

Special thanks to the Ottawa writing community, especially Charlotte Helen Schrock Robertson, Adam Meisner, Frances Boyle, David O'Meara, Sean Wilson, Ellen Chang-Richardson, Jean Van Loon, Chris Johnson, Amanda Earl, Manahil Bandukwala, and Rob McLennan. Thank you to the Canada Council for the Arts and the Ontario Arts Council for believing in new writers and their ideas.

Dad, thank you for your prayers. Mom, thank you for the stars. Claire and Catherine, thank you for giving me a place to hang my heart. Charles, Heidi, and Julia, you are why I write stories, and Nathan, I'm glad you smiled at me that time.

SARA POWER is a storyteller from Labrador, and a former artillery officer in the Canadian Forces. Her stories have appeared in journals across Canada, the US, and the UK, and most recently in *Best Canadian Stories 2024*. Sara was a finalist for the RBC/PEN Canada New Voices Award and received a nomination for a National Magazine Award in the fiction category. Her stories have been recognized with fiction awards from *The Malahat Review, Riddle Fence, The Toronto Star, Prairie Fire Magazine,* and *The New Quarterly*. Sara completed a Bachelor of Science from The Royal Military College of Canada and a Master of Fine Arts from The University of British Columbia. She is an alumna of the Disquiet Literary Program in Lisbon, the Banff Centre Writing Studio Program, the Middlebury Bread Loaf Writers' Conference, and the International Literary Seminars in Kenya. Sara lives in Ottawa with her husband, three children, and hound dog.